The
Connemara
Stallion

Also by Ann Henning

The Connemara Whirlwind

The Connemara Champion

The
Connemara
Stallion

Ann Henning

POOLBEG

All incidents and characters in this book are purely fictitious and any resemblance to real characters, living or dead, or to actual events, is entirely accidental.

First published in 1991 by
Poolbeg Press Ltd,
123 Baldoyle Industrial Estate,
Dublin 13,
Ireland
E-mail: **poolbeg@poolbeg.com**
www.poolbeg.com
Reissued 2001

A catalogue record for this book is available from the British Library.

ISBN 1 85371 158 6

Cover Photography by Michael Edwards
Cover design by Vivid
Printed by The Guernsey Press Ltd,
Vale, Guernsey, Channel Islands.

For Shane

Contents

Cuaifeach the Stallion

1

ot many twelve-year-old girls in this world keep their own stallion. Doreen Joyce of Inishnee was certainly the only one in Connemara. "And I'm beginning to see why," the girl sighed to herself, as she trudged across a rough field one icy cold morning in January.

It was dark; the sun arrived late in this westerly part of Ireland. Remnants of the previous night's gale still raged around her, tore at the armful of hay and straw she was carrying, sent specks of stalks and seed whirling like a cloud around her head. It was too dark to see the tiny particles but she felt them as they hit her face. Now and then there was a crackle of ice breaking under her feet. Finding the path leading to the shed at the far end of the field was no problem. She knew it well enough, having walked this way and back twice a day every day for months.

That misty day in October when she was able to buy Cuaifeach, the pony of her dreams, at the big fair at Maam Cross, she had truly believed that she would never again be unhappy. The future had stretched ahead of her as an endless series of beautiful rose-coloured days: warm sunshine, gentle south-westerly winds, the whole of the world open for her and her pony to explore together. Reality had turned out to have little in common with this vision. All that her life with Cuaifeach had amounted to so far was this never-ending haul of hay and straw across a boggy wet field, early mornings and late afternoons, in all kinds of weather, with nothing better at the end of it than a murky shed containing a disgruntled pony.

It was not as if Doreen was a stranger to hard work. Like most Connemara children she had been used to giving a hand at the farm for as long as she could remember. There were many things even a small child could do to help: feed the chickens, drive the cows, bring tea to the men working on the bog. Such work they often preferred to playing. It made them feel useful, as if the grown-ups couldn't quite manage without them.

If they ever complained, they were soon reminded of the life children in Connemara had had in the old days. Doreen had often heard the story of her grandmother, who had gone to work in Mullins Hotel in Roundstone at the age of fourteen. Her working day had begun at five o'clock in the morning, when she had to climb Errisbeg, the huge sprawling mountain behind the village, to find the hotel's cow, milk it and bring back the pail in time for the hotel breakfast. The desperate hours she had spent running over that mountain, barefoot in the pouring rain, searching for the wayward cow! Anyone who has ever been on Errisbeg mountain, let alone tried to locate a stray animal there, will appreciate the difficulty of her task. And that was only the start of a long working day.

No, Doreen thought, it wasn't the hard work of looking after the colt that she minded. As far as she was concerned, no effort in the world would have been too great if it was a matter of keeping her pony happy. But that was the whole problem: Cuaifeach was not happy. He was miserable.

If only they had been able to have him gelded as soon as he was bought! That had

indeed been the plan. Castration would have
made him unable to sire foals and the level of
male hormone in his blood would have been
reduced to make him docile and content. That,
anyhow, was how the vet had explained it to
Doreen, though she found it hard to believe
that a slight operation could have brought
about such a complete change of character.
Still, the main thing was that as a gelding he
would have posed no threat to other people's
mares. He could have been let out of the shed
to run around freely without any risk of
unwanted foals all over the place. As a stallion
he had to be kept in isolation. Doreen had been
warned in no uncertain terms about the stiff
penalties for stallion owners who let their
animals stray. The pony could be taken away
by the guards, even be put down. Ponybreeding
was a serious business in these parts, and there
were laws and regulations to protect the purity
of the Connemara breed. Only specially
approved stallions could be used if the offspring
was to be recognised by the official stud book.
And while a pure-bred Connemara pony could
be worth a lot of money, you'd be hard put to
get any price for a foal without proper breeding
papers. For this reason alone, there was no
sympathy and no mercy for those who broke

the rules.

In these circumstances, it was obviously essential that Cuaifeach should be gelded without delay. But when the vet was called in, he had advised strongly against it. November was too late in the year to geld a colt, he said; it would take too much out of him. He could get sick, his growth could be stunted. Much better to keep him entire over the winter and have the operation done in the spring. Much better for the pony.

Doreen did not need much persuasion. She was secretly relieved that the surgery had been postponed. The vet assured her that, undertaken at the right time, it was only a minor procedure; with modern methods there were rarely any complications. But Doreen still had her misgivings. The doctor had said much the same thing when her Mam was taken in to have her gall-bladder removed and she still wasn't well, though months had passed since she came home. No one could explain what had gone wrong, why her mother did not recover. All Doreen knew was that the operation somehow seemed to have been the cause of it.

Then the vet had gone on to explain that Cuaifeach would have to be kept in for the winter. "You're a lucky boy," he said, patting

the neck of the pony who looked him suspiciously up and down. "No winter storms for
you this year. You'll be pampered and waited
upon like a king in his castle."

The vet, of course, had no way of knowing—
any more than Doreen at the time—that if
there was one thing Cuaifeach could not stand,
it was being shut in. Looking back, Doreen
thought, she really ought to have guessed as
much. A pony generally referred to as the
wildest colt in Connemara, how could they have
expected him to settle down to being under lock
and key? Wasn't he born under the *cuaifeach*
itself, and named after it, the wicked fairy wind
that took no heed of anything standing in its
way? Try containing a whirlwind in a shed—if
it didn't succeed in blowing the place to pieces,
it would...it would simply expire.

The girl quickened her step. The day was
beginning to break in all its greyness and she
could see the dim outline of the shed. Cuaifeach
would never be able to wreck that solid
structure. It had been a house once, home to a
large family. It had a proper chimney and
windows on all but the north wall, though there
was no glass in them. They were boarded up
for the winter to stop the high winds lifting
the roof off from inside.

Cuaifeach, hearing her footsteps, was calling impatiently for his breakfast. At least he hadn't gone off his food; on the contrary, he had given himself to compensatory eating. It was as if he could never get enough. Doreen's post office savings were dwindling rapidly, eaten up in the shape of hay and nuts. But she was determined that he should never go hungry.

She opened the door of the shed carefully against the wind and shut it again behind her before groping in the dark for the torch hanging up on a nail. The yellow beam fell on the floor. From the shadows the stallion glared at her, his ears in his usual unfriendly position halfway back.

"Oh, don't feel so sorry for yourself!" Doreen burst out. "Here I come, through the ice and wind, just to keep you fed and watered, and you haven't even the sense to be grateful. What would you say if I didn't come at all, I wonder?"

Cuaifeach snatched at her armful of hay and, presumably by mistake, caught her little finger.

"And don't be so damned bold!"

Doreen didn't normally swear, but she felt this was the only language that Cuaifeach in his present frame of mind would understand.

In reply he snatched again. Doreen smacked

him hard on the nose, and he retreated sulkily.

"There's a good boy," she said, as he stood aside to let her remove last night's empty haynet and refill it. Then, as he attacked the hay, she went on to clean out the dung and prepare a fresh bed of straw. It was easy to keep the place clean, Cuaifeach was a neat pony who used different corners of the shed for his different functions. As usual she chatted to him while she worked:

"I can tell you no other pony has such a fine stable to live in. Look—you've even got a fireplace. I wouldn't complain if I had to spend the winter here. Who'd want to be out in this awful weather anyway?"

Cuaifeach took no notice of her, just munched away greedily. To him it was all nonsense, Doreen thought; of course he wanted to be out, it was all he was pining for. He didn't mind the weather as long as he could run around a field, greet the new day with a frisky gallop, climb the highest rock to gaze out over the wide open spaces, call out towards the Big Bens and hear the distant reply from the wild herds roaming there. He wanted to have freedom of movement, like generations of Connemara ponies before him, like hundreds of ponies around him at this very moment.

Freedom if only to roll in the mud, doze in the midday sunshine, nibble at lichens and pale winter grass.

But it was not to be. For the time being, Cuaifeach was a prisoner. And worst of all was the fact that she, Doreen, she who loved him more than anything, whose only wish was to see him happy, had to act as his jailor.

Last weekend she had gone all the way over to Ballyconneely to see her grand-uncle Christy and ask his advice. Couldn't she let Cuaifeach out in the field for an hour or two now and then? At weekends, when she could stay with him? After all, it wasn't the breeding season and most of the mares in Inishnee were in foal anyway.

But Uncle Christy had shaken his head sombrely. "With another horse you might have chanced it," he said, meaning by the word "horse" a pony stallion. "But not this one. He's too mad. I can tell he is one of them fellers what lose their head when they see a skirt. There's no accounting for what he might do."

"Skirt?" Doreen asked, confused.

"Oh well," said Christy, remembering that mares don't wear skirts, "you know what I mean...females."

He uttered the word with some distaste,

being as he was a confirmed old bachelor.

"You think he'd go for the mares?"

"Like a bullet," Christy replied. "He'd be over the fence and across the causeway, up the mountains before you had time to shut the door after him. And once he spotted the mares roaming up there, he'd never come back. No one would ever be able to catch him. He'd have to be shot."

Doreen had armed herself with a number of suggestions, like having him on a rope, or building up the fences, even putting him in the garden. But she never had a chance to put these proposals forward. Christy had dismissed the idea and was off on another tack, reminiscing about the past the way old people do. Oh, the days when he and his friend Patsy, the official stallion-keeper for Ballyconneely, used to take the stallion up to the wild herds in the mountains! There would be fifty or sixty mares running together, never caught by man, and they had to be rounded up and driven into a pen. Then the stallion was brought along on a rope at least a hundred feet long...

"He spent days in there," Christy told his grand-niece, excited at the memory. "I was the one holding on to the other end of the rope. That was work fit for a man, I can tell you!"

"Why did you have to hold on to him?"
Doreen asked innocently. "Why didn't you just
let him off into the pen?"

"Well that just shows how much a girl
understands about stallions!" Christy snorted.
"Let him loose amongst sixty mares? Don't you
know, he'd be there to this day!"

Doreen looked at Cuaifeach. With the worst
of his hunger appeased, he was beginning to
settle a bit. How handsome he looked in his
sleek shiny coat, so unlike the rough shaggy
ponies who spent the winter out of doors! If
only she didn't have to see that terrible
resentment, or rather, sadness in his eye!

"It's only another three months," she told
him. "What's three months in a whole lifetime?
Then, Cuaifeach, spring will be upon us, you'll
have your operation, and after that you can
run around to your heart's content. Just think
of all the lovely green grass you'll be eating!
And then it will be summer...the sun will
shine, and we'll go riding together. We'll go for
gallops on the beach and we'll swim and...Oh,
I promise you, we'll have lots of fun, I'll see to
it that we do! I know you're awful bored,
Cuaifeach, I know you're sorry you came to me.
But I'll make up for it, I really will. Before you
know what has happened, you'll be as happy

again as ever, I swear!"

The pony had turned away from the haynet and was looking at her intently as if he wanted to understand her words but couldn't quite make it. In the end her pleading tone must have got to him for he came up and rubbed his face gently against her stomach, something he hadn't done for a long time.

"Oh Cuaifeach," she whispered, scratching the base of his ear, "wouldn't I give anything just to set you free?"

The desire to open the door was so great that she had to remind herself that she was responsible not only for protecting other people's mares from Cuaifeach. She also had to protect him from the dangers lurking outside. There was a very real danger that another pony had recently fallen victim to.

❋❋❋

Doreen and her brother Tom had come home from school the previous day to find the lights on in the cottage, a fire blazing in the kitchen and a pot of potatoes boiling away merrily over it. Their Mam was up and dressed, busy making tea, and there was a lovely smell of fresh soda bread. It was almost like it used to be in the old days, when their Dad and their elder brothers and sisters were still there, when the cottage was like a real home, alive with food and chatter and with a fire that never went out. Nowadays the two remaining children often came home to a cold grate. Their mother would be in bed in the dark back room, and they had to get their own dinner.

The reason for the sudden change was a visitor seated at the kitchen table. They knew him well. His name was Johnny Conneely, though everyone referred to him under his nickname Johnny Tass, given to him by some humorous person after the Soviet news agency. Johnny was a great one for passing on information. He seemed to know everything that was going on in Connemara, sometimes he even knew things before they had happened. His tidings weren't always a hundred per cent accurate; Johnny was not above filling in a few missing details, and his love of a good story occasionally led him to invent a little extra gossip. However there was always a measure of truth in his reports and everybody knew that they could not be readily dismissed. As someone had once put it: "The problem with Johnny Tass is, half of what he says is true, but you never know which half."

This day he was standing in for the postman, who had gone down with flu. This temporary task, regularly undertaken by Johnny, was an absolute godsend to him, as it provided a ready-made excuse to visit all the households in the area and form a complete picture of things as they were—or were made out to be. He dutifully went to every house, whether or not there was mail to deliver, and spent a little while gossiping in each place. The later it was in the day, the more news he had to impart, and so his visits became more extended as time wore on. People looked forward to his calls for the wealth of information they brought and overlooked the fact that their mail was delivered hours behind schedule.

Whenever the regular postman did not turn up on time, it could be safely concluded that a visit from Johnny could be expected, and the housewives of Connemara, like Roisin Joyce, Tom's and Doreen's mother, set about making cakes and preparing tea, anything to keep him at their table for as long as possible.

At the moment Johnny was sitting silently at the table, thoughtfully stirring his tea. This was unusual for him but then his silence was more like a dramatic pause in anticipation of delivering a sensation.

Mrs Joyce put a plateful of the homemade bread in front of him.

"You were on the verge of telling me somewhat," she prompted him. She looked bright and cheerful and her cheeks were flushed, from excitement as much as from the heat of the fire.

Johnny gave an expressive sigh and waited for the children to settle next to him. Then he said, slowly: "Bernard's mare was killed."

"Killed?" Doreen exclaimed. "That lovely grey mare?"

Johnny nodded. It was obvious that he, too, was distressed by the news for he was not normally a man of few words.

"I saw her only yesterday," Doreen went on. "She was heavy in foal."

"That's right," said Johnny. "To Abbeyleix Owen," he added morosely, as if this somehow made the matter worse.

"How was she killed?" Tom asked.

"On the road, just in front of Bernard's cottage. He heard the crash in the dead of night. By the time he got out, all that was there was the glass of a shattered windscreen and the mare stone dead beside it."

"Some drunk, of course," Mrs Joyce muttered.

"Sure now," Johnny agreed. "But no one will

be able to prove it."

"That's terrible," Doreen said in a trembling voice. "That someone could do such a thing, and then just drive off, without checking if the mare was suffering."

"How is Bernard taking it?" Roisin Joyce enquired.

"Devastated," Johnny replied. "I never saw a man so devastated. That mare was his pride and joy."

"Did he call the guards?" Tom wanted to know. "Surely they can work out who done it?"

But Johnny said no, this was not a case for the guards.

"Why not?" Doreen demanded. "Drunks like that shouldn't be allowed to go around killing people's ponies!"

Johnny, well informed as ever, explained that there was a new law: anyone who let an animal stray on to the road was responsible for any accidents it caused. So Bernard could be getting himself into trouble.

"Perhaps we could try and find out who it was," Tom suggested to his sister.

There was no need for that, Johnny told them, a note of pride creeping into his voice. "Don't forget," he said, "that I've spent the day going round the country. And I can tell you this: only one car had a broken windscreen."

Then, with a modest smile, he went on to tell them that he had it on reliable grounds that the owner of the said car had been seen leaving a certain bar in Roundstone late the previous night.

"Oh Johnny!" Mrs Joyce exclaimed admiringly, "you're like one of them detectives on television!"

"Who was it?" Doreen asked grimly.

But Johnny wouldn't tell them, he could only offer them a clue: the man drove a blue Toyota with a brown side door.

That was no help to them.

"All right then," Johnny continued, "why does it have a brown door? Because it's no more than three weeks since the night he crashed his car into a tree in Ballinahinch Forest!"

"I know who it is!" Tom cried. "I heard about that! It's Pad—"

"No names!" Johnny interrupted. "The less said the better. And whatever you do, don't say anything to Bernard!"

"You haven't told him?" Mrs Joyce asked, astonished.

"He wouldn't get it out of me, if he had me on a rack," Johnny vowed.

Doreen stood up. There were sparks flying

from her eyes. "And you're supposed to be Bernard's friend!" she cried out. "Some friend who protects a useless drunk who ought to be in prison for what he done—"

"Now wait a minute," said Johnny good-humouredly. "Of course I'm Bernard's friend. That's the whole reason why I don't want him to know."

"He has a right to know!" Doreen cried.

"And if I told him, what do you think would happen?" Johnny asked her.

"He'd be going straight over to that—that villain and give him what he deserves! Bernard is no coward. And he's the strongest man I know!"

"That's just it," said Johnny. "If Bernard was let into that house, he'd come out of it a murderer. And then who'd be going to prison?"

It took a few moments for the argument to sink in. Then they all understood and there was no more to say.

"So you see," Johnny concluded, "Bernard must never know."

❋❋❋

All this was very much on Doreen's mind, as she stroked her own pony's silky warm coat, ran her frozen fingers through his wild black mane. Poor Bernard and his lovely grey mare.

"One thing I'll tell you," she said to Cuaifeach. "You may be killed with boredom—but it's a whole lot worse to be killed dead."

2

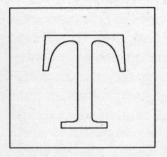hroughout history, people in Connemara have found ways to thrive in spite of their harsh living conditions. Sheep and cattle were reared on the meagre hillsides and the lean meat, strong hides and thick fleeces were shipped out to faraway countries as early as the Middle Ages. The overseas trade occupies many people to this day: from the intrepid fishermen who brave the seas to catch salmon and shellfish for the most discerning continental palates, to the housewives who spend dark winter evenings knitting sweaters that will go on sale in the fashionable stores of London and New York.

But not only has Connemara always had much to offer other parts of the world: for such an isolated region, it is also, by tradition, remarkably open to influence from outside. Foreigners are met with an enthusiastic welcome, their ideas taken in with keen interest and, if proven to be sound, soon assimilated into the Connemara way of life.

So it was in the early decades of this century, when officials from England and the East arrived on the scene, informing the local people that the rough ponies roaming their mountains possessed rare and sought-after qualities that were well worth preserving. Ponies were to be caught and brought down for inspection and registration, and breeding was to be strictly controlled. The inhabitants of Connemara decided to give their full support to the project, and we all know the result: the foundation of one of the world's most celebrated pure pony breeds.

Then there are of course all the regular incidents of helpful strangers turning up and telling the natives of better, more efficient ways of sailing their boats, feeding their stock, catching their fish. Their advice is usually received with politeness and an open mind— not even the wildest suggestion is dismissed out of hand but given the benefit of the doubt. Until, that is, it can be put to the test—and preferably in public, in regattas, pony shows or angling competitions. Great interest is shown each time a clever foreigner pitches his methods against the survival skills developed over many Connemara generations. And there is no end to the mirth when—as often happens—the expert stranger comes to grief. On the other hand: if he should prove himself to be successful, he will be granted all the respect and credit due to him.

In this vein, a small crowd had gathered one breezy morning in March at the farmyard of the O'Briens' homestead in Murvey. Word had got out that Andy and Jake O'Brien were about to practise their brilliant horsemanship on the redoubtable Cuaifeach. The two brothers had arrived from America a few months earlier to claim the inheritance left to them by their uncle—one of the largest farms in this barren area. Much of the winter evenings they had spent in pubs from Clifden to Carna, boasting about their work as cowboys on ranches in the American Mid-West. There were tales of hair-raising round-ups of savage colts, of breakneck gallops across the wide prairie, of rodeos that left not only the horses broken but also most of the riders' bones. With the obvious exception of the O'Briens, of course—they never came to any harm! There seemed to be no horse-coping trick invented that they had not mastered.

And now Christy Joyce, grand-uncle of the girl Doreen, had entrusted them with the task of transforming Cuaifeach, the Connemara Whirlwind, into a quiet, well-mannered child's riding pony. The crowd could hardly wait for the spectacle to begin.

Cuaifeach was still a stallion. The plan had been to have him gelded in April, then give him a few weeks to recover before any attempt was made to ride him. But when Christy went over to see the Joyce family at Easter, he was astounded to see how the colt had come on over the winter. He had grown bone, a good seven inches below the knee, he had developed an impressive sloping shoulder and solid round hind-quarters. As the pony turned to look at Christy, his neck proudly arched, the stamp of his mother Veronica, the champion mare, was all over him. Isn't it mighty, the old man thought to himself, how good blood will out?

Then Doreen had said something about having him gelded. How much longer? she wanted to know. Could it be done any sooner, seeing he was in such good condition?

"You're out of yer mind, girl," was Christy's reply. "You don't go gelding a feller like this one. He has to be brought up for inspection in

May. Don't you know, they may pass him as a stallion!"

And the old man was off in a dream, with himself turning up at the stallion inspection at Maam Cross parading this beautiful colt in front of an admiring crowd. "Look at old Christy's horse," they would say, "we thought he was out of it altogether, but look what he's got now." The inspectors, of course, would be equally impressed...oh, the honour of it! It was forty-three years since the first and last time that Christy had ever had a stallion approved, but he had never forgotten the glory of that moment.

Only the accursed girl had different ideas. "What would I with a stallion?" she said. "All I want is a pony to ride."

Christy had to apply all his powers of persuasion, list the arguments one by one: the pony, even after being gelded, would be much more valuable if he had once been passed by the inspection committee—it was like a quality seal. Moreover, if you possessed a decent colt, it was your duty to present him. If he was considered good enough, his blood must be carried forward, to the benefit of the whole breed. And then the distinction—to be down in the stud book as a registered stallion owner—that was really something.

Doreen did not even seem to think it worth considering. Exasperated, Christy had to resort to compromises: they could have him gelded shortly after the inspection. If he was approved, he could cover a couple of mares in rapid succession before his brief stud career came to an end. That way the blood-line would be preserved, and Doreen would still have her riding pony. (And I'd have the honour, Christy mused to himself.)

But the girl said it would leave breaking the pony too late. Her intention was to have him ready and riding in time for the school holidays.

It was then that Christy had his bright idea—one that she simply could not counter. He would have the colt broken for her professionally, at his own expense, before the inspection. That would get him riding sooner than expected. How was that?

"She's not going riding a stallion!" Mrs Joyce put in.

"He can be gelded in June," Christy reassured her. "She can leave off riding him until then."

Doreen still had reservations: "Won't he be too difficult to break while he's still a stallion?"

Christy grinned. "Don't you worry yerself,

girl. The fellers I have in mind are well able for him!"

***

Cuaifeach was standing in the middle of the O'Briens' farmyard, looking casually around him. The yard was rough and extremely dirty: half the neighbourhood's heads of cattle had been through the crush the day before for TB testing. Farmyards are a rare luxury in Connemara, and anyone lucky enough to possess a crush is expected to share it with those who don't.

It was, in fact, thanks to this enclosed area that the O'Brien brothers had been able to take on the job of breaking a stallion. Now, to confine the space further, they were placing bales of straw in a ring around the pony. He watched them with a puzzled look. To him they probably appeared rather strange, as they swaggered around in their large cowboy hats, Western boots and spotted neckerchiefs. As Seamus Lee, one of the onlookers, put it: only the holsters were missing.

The ring of straw completed, the O'Briens stepped back a little, sizing up their charge, as it were.

"What'cha think?" Andy asked his brother in a low voice.

Jake cracked a long whip in the air. "A walkover," he replied under his breath.

"Cuaifeach seems to be in good form," Christy announced cheerily to his mates over by the gate. He was in good form himself, seeing that everything was working out according to his plan. The transport from Inishnee had gone without a hitch although Doreen had had to give him a hand loading the pony before she went off to school. Then she had threatened to come along and watch but that Christy had managed to ward off, saying that she mustn't miss classes but could come along afterwards. Otherwise she might have made a nuisance of herself, interfered with the lads' methods. Girls knew nothing about stallions, all this mollycoddling, it was enough to ruin a horse.

"How come he's so quiet?" asked one man disappointedly. He had never seen Cuaifeach before but, having heard a lot about him, had expected something more like a raging bull.

"You just wait, Festy," said Christy, anxious to protect the colt's reputation. "You just wait."

But inwardly he wondered himself over the pony's sudden meekness. It did, in fact, have a perfectly good explanation, though no one, not even Doreen, knew it. Once the winter storms were over, the girl had taken the shutters off the windows of Cuaifeach's shed to enable him to see out. After so many months of solitary confinement, the colt had been overwhelmed by this prospect and had kept watch at each window in turn, fascinated by the movement of birds and rabbits, cats and donkeys, and even the odd mare in the distance. The activity had so absorbed him that he had lost out on his sleep, especially now that the days were getting longer. The reason he was so subdued was, quite simply, that he was dog tired.

"This kind of work I find very interesting," said Johnny Tass, who, naturally, was on site taking note of every detail. "I remember my Dad breaking mares for the cart. He'd get them about this time of year when they were weak and hungry. There wasn't much resistance in them then."

"There's nothing weak or hungry about that one," said another man, indicating Cuaifeach.

"Oh no, this is a different match altogether," said Jimmy Mac, one of the O'Briens' nearest neighbours, who was easily impressed and an ardent supporter of the brothers. "This will be more like what you see in films."

"The Wild West has arrived in Connemara!" called Seamus Lee. "Hurrah!"

They all laughed.

The brothers had tied the end of Cuaifeach's rope halter to the gate post. It was so tight that he could hardly move his head. Andy now produced a very elegant leather bridle, jangling with gleaming ironmongery. The bit was a formidable twisted bar, more severe than any bit normally seen or used in Connemara.

"They need that sort of thing to control a horse out on the prairie," Jimmy Mac told the others admiringly.

"But hardly in O'Briens' yard," quipped Seamus Lee.

Andy, after some difficulty, as Cuaifeach would not stand still, had the bridle over his nose and was trying to insert the large bit.

"Open yer mouth, stupid," he said.

Cuaifeach obligingly did as he was told. But then he closed his mouth again just as quickly. There was a loud yelp and Andy withdrew, nursing a bleeding finger.

"You jerk!" Jake hissed. "You were supposed to stick the bit in his mouth, not yer blooming finger!"

He picked up the bridle, which had dropped onto the ground, angrily brushed off the worst dirt and got hold of the stallion's head. However, this time the pony would not open his mouth at all. He clenched his jaws determinedly, pretending not to notice Jake's attempts to prise them open.

A titter went through the crowd. Jake threw down the bridle.

"We're used to dealing with horses," he said in a loud voice. "These ponies are more like asses!"

His brother had disappeared for a moment but now he came back carrying a sack and a magnificent Western saddle, heavily embossed and mounted with silver. His right index finger was wrapped in a clumsy bandage.

"Give it here," said Jake, snatching the sack from him.

Cuaifeach, expecting to find something nice to eat, inquisitively stuck his head into it. He must have been surprised when the sack was pulled up over his head and neck, but he showed no reaction. The crowd stared, open-mouthed.

"This is a kinda precaution," Jake explained to them. "Some high-strung horses go bananas when they first see a saddle. But it's hardly necessary when you break in asses."

Together the brothers placed the huge

saddle on Cuaifeach's back. It landed with a great thud, obviously very heavy. The pony was unperturbed. On a sign from Jake, Andy peeled back the sack. Cuaifeach yawned.

"Wild and dangerous," Andy sneered. "He, he."

"Take it away!" Jake ordered irritably. "I told you there was no need for it."

Then he leant over the saddle, putting as much as possible of his own weight onto it. The stallion remained unconcerned. He seemed to be more interested in the view over Dog's Bay.

"What'd you say we're getting for this job?" Andy hissed.

"Three of Christy's ewes, picked by ourselves," Jake chuckled.

"I'll almost be ashamed to claim them," Andy grinned.

"Come on," said Jake, "untie that rope and I'll have myself a little ride. It will be the fastest breaking job anyone ever saw this side of the Atlantic."

The rope halter was fixed up so that it also provided a pair of reins. Then, whistling the opening bars of "The Yellow Rose of Texas", Jake put his foot in the bulky leather stirrup and with a swift movement swung himself up into the saddle.

It was then, as he was in mid-air, in that split second, that the crowd noticed a change in Cuaifeach. It was as if the pony suddenly switched on to full alert: his gaze sharpened, the ears were pointed, his whole stance became poised as for instant action. What then happened came as a surprise to no one but the two O'Briens—but then, Jake had his head turned the other way, and Andy was intent on watching his brother. Cuaifeach's timing was absolute perfection: the moment Jake's behind went down in the saddle, his own went up in the air. The hero from the Wild West was catapulted in an arc across his own farmyard, landing, predictably, on one of the cowpats that all but covered the ground.

The crowd over at the gate howled with laughter.

"Some film!" someone cried.

"Better than Laurel and Hardy!" Seamus Lee cheered.

Cuaifeach looked as if he was laughing, too, as he took himself off in a wild fandango. The bales of straw proved no obstacle—he soon had them scattered in all directions. Cow dung splattered from under his hooves, and Jake's smart Stetson, which had come off in the fall, was trampled into the shape of a pancake. The yard looked, in Johnny Tass's words, as if it had indeed been "hit by the cuaifeach".

Andy had rushed to his brother's aid. "You okay?" he asked breathlessly.

"Of course I'm okay!" Jake snarled, scrambling to his feet. "Go catch the goddamn ass!" He turned and pointed in the pony's direction. Then a strangled shriek rose from his throat. "Hey! For Chrissake, stop him!"

Cuaifeach, in the dirtiest patch over at the crush, had gone down on his knees in preparation for a long good roll. Jake was jumping round desperately, looking for his whip. It was apparent that his fall had left him with a bad limp.

"Get him!" he roared at Andy, who made an awkward lunge at the halter. In response Cuaifeach rolled away from him, onto his back. There was a crunch of broken wood underneath his half-ton of horseflesh. But he obviously found the Western saddle uncomfortable to roll on, for he soon got to his feet again and shook himself vigorously to get rid of the strange contraption on his back. All he managed was to set it sliding down his side.

"Eight hundred dollars!" Jake groaned. "I paid eight hundred bucks for that saddle, only to have it mangled by an ass!"

Giving vent to his fury, he lashed his whip in the direction of Cuaifeach's head. As might have been expected, that set the pony galloping again. Jake slumped down on a bale of straw, reached for his mud-stained hat and glumly tried to box it back into shape.

The stallion had suddenly pulled up short in front of the O'Briens' big shed. One of the brothers' main jobs during the winter had been to install a large window in the wall facing the yard. It had been hard work cutting through the stone wall and then fitting the window but once it was done, the brothers were very pleased with the light, airy space they had created.

Cuaifeach was looking at the window as if he couldn't believe his eyes.

"If they haven't a mare in the shed!" said Seamus Lee. "That, I would say, was not well-considered!"

The stallion was indeed making romantic overtures to someone he saw in the shed. He gave out foolish, contented noises, like a man on a desert island who suddenly finds the woman of his dreams washed up on the shore.

"Don't let him get in to her!" Christy warned the brothers. "He's not registered yet!"

"To who?" Andy asked, confused.

"But it's another colt!" Johnny Tass exclaimed. "Look—he's going to fight him!"

All faces turned towards Cuaifeach. He had discovered his mistake: the gorgeous creature facing him was not a mare at all but another stallion, a rival competing for his territory! There was only one possible response to such impudence: immediate attack, using front hooves.

The broad windowpane shattered into smithereens, and bits of broken glass rained over the cowpats. Cuaifeach stared perplexedly into the empty shed.

"Mind the other colt!" Seamus Lee shouted.

"There *is* no other colt!" Jake snapped.

"But he definitely saw someone in there..." Jimmy Mac began timidly.

"He saw his own reflection in the glass!" Jake roared. "God almighty, I believe you're all as stupid as he is! What are you doing here anyways? How can you expect us to get any work done with you lot gawping at us?"

He turned round, only to find himself nose to nose with Cuaifeach, who had come creeping up behind him.

"Is he injured?" Christy called anxiously.

"Not he," Jake replied bitterly, more concerned with the damage done to the saddle.

"There's not a scratch on him."

The same could not be said about Andy, who, starting to pick up the broken glass, had cut his hand—the same hand that had previously been bitten—and was bleeding profusely. He was standing stock still, staring in horror at the wound.

"Do you need any help?" Seamus Lee enquired.

There was a thump when Andy fell to the ground. He had fainted.

"We've had all the help we need from you lot!" Jake shouted. "Now will you excuse me while I revive my brother?"

❋❋❋

A little later, in King's Bar in Roundstone, Christy gave in to a fit of gloom over a pint of stout.

"If this doesn't work out," he confided dejectedly to Johnny Tass, "I don't know what I'll do. The girl is so contrary, she may well go off and have him gelded before the inspection."

"She won't if you plead with her," was Johnny's reply.

"Plead? With a girleen like that? I'd rather die," Christy declared categorically.

"Come on," said Johnny Tass, who could never resist teasing the old bachelor. "If you're all set on it, you may even try going down on your knees."

"I'll do no such thing," Christy vowed. "I have managed for seventy-eight years without having to beg anything of a girl, and I am not going to start now."

Johnny Tass wasn't listening. His attention had been claimed elsewhere.

"Jesus, Mary," he said hoarsely between his teeth. "This will have to be stopped."

Christy's gaze followed his until it settled on a pair in a corner: it was Bernard, who had lost his lovely grey mare, and a shifty-looking character called Paddy, who everyone except Bernard knew was the one who had killed her. Now the two men were engaged in what looked like friendly conversation. Bernard was even patting Paddy on the back.

"Let me get you a drink," he offered jovially. "What'll you have?"

"Er..." Paddy replied, his shifty gaze flickering all over the place. "I...er...don't take the drink any more."

"Is that so?" said Bernard with warm interest. "You've given it up?"

"I have," Paddy mumbled. "I'm in the AA. But

I'll get one for you. What are you drinking?"

"A large Jameson, if you insist," Bernard said good-naturedly, and then he turned and winked at his friends, which only increased their disconcertion.

With Paddy queuing up at the bar, Johnny Tass invented a pretext to take Bernard outside. They went into a narrow laneway beside the bar where they wouldn't be overheard. "Bernard," Johnny started solemnly, "there's something you ought to know."

The other man smiled broadly. "I couldn't help seeing the look on yer faces in there. Did you really think I didn't know?"

Johnny was flabbergasted. "You do know?"

"Of course," said Bernard. "I found out the day after it happened. You should know, in this place you couldn't sneeze and keep it a secret."

"But you were talking to him! Offering him a drink, even!"

Bernard still looked amused. "I tell you now," he said, "I thought long and hard about it. When I was first told, I got the axe out. But the wife stopped me and a good thing that was, because the one to suffer most would have been myself. So instead I thought, what if I do nothing? Won't it make him feel rotten, being left there to stew, not knowing whether I know, and wondering what I might do to him the day I find out? It will be with him for as long as he lives, and the friendlier I am towards him, the worse he will feel, right?"

"So that's what you're up to?" Johnny said, duly impressed. This would be a good story to relay.

"I think it's working," Bernard resumed. "Didn't you hear, he's off the drink. He has joined Alcoholics Anonymous. He won't be doing any more drunken driving."

"Bernard," said Johnny Tass sincerely, "I'd take my hat off to you, if I had one."

"No need," said Bernard. "Just don't give the game away."

            ❀❀❀

Meanwhile, the O'Brien brothers were sitting at their kitchen table. Andy was still feeling wonky, though he had picked up a little after several cups of strong tea and a large corned-beef sandwich. His right hand was heavily bandaged, and he kept it resting on the table. The cut was still throbbing, although Jake had assured him that it was "a mere scratch".

"I don't feel like doing any more," he muttered.

"We've got to have another go!" Jake insisted. "Don't you see, our whole future in this place depends on it!"

"It's raining," said Andy.

Jake looked out over the bay. Dark storm clouds were gathering out there and the sea was leaden. Overland a fine grey mist was rising, a light rain falling.

"Come on!" he said. "You're not afraid of him? He's only an ass."

"Is he?" said Andy gloomily.

Jake got up. "Come along," he commanded, secure in the knowledge that his brother never seriously opposed him. "We might as well get it over with!"

They agreed to lunge Cuaifeach to get rid of any surplus energy before trying to ride him again. "Ringing him", Slim, their idolised American employer, had called it. Jake got Andy to hold the rope in his good hand while he himself went behind the pony with the whip. But Cuaifeach had no intention of running around in circles—he simply could not see the point.

"We mustn't give in to him!" Jake declared, cracking the whip furiously around his hocks and then giving a good wallop over his backside. "Go on, you brute! Go on!"

Now Cuaifeach did not have a record of being a vicious pony. Wild, of course, exuberantly so, but not vindictive. However, there were certain things that he would not stand for, such as being beaten when, in his own view, he had done no wrong. Against such assaults he felt obliged to retaliate. So when Jake's whip landed once more on his now rather tender behind, he decided that enough was enough and turned round, ears back and teeth bared, to chase the offender away.

Jake, terrified, staggered off on his injured knee, but Cuaifeach kept pursuing him around the yard, finally describing the circles they had previously tried so hard to achieve. Andy came rushing after him, holding on to the rope, trying unsuccessfully to haul him back. Suddenly Jake threw himself sidewards, out of the stallion's path but, as it happened, into that of his brother. Andy couldn't stop in time but bumped straight into him. The brothers collapsed in the muck. Cuaifeach narrowly avoided landing on top of them.

"This," Jake panted, "must be the first time ever that I've been ringed by a horse."

"By an ass," Andy corrected him.

"At least we didn't have an audience this time," Jake sighed, and all of a sudden, the brothers burst out laughing.

"Let's try something else," Andy suggested.

The saddle turned out to be battered but still serviceable. They put it back on the pony, who didn't seem to mind.

"I'll say one thing for him," Andy conceded. "He's not of a nervous disposition."

"Just as well," Jake replied, "for it's your turn to ride him."

"Mine?" Andy cried. "But I'm injured!"

"So am I, for Chrissake! All right," Jake added, seeing how pale his brother had become, "if it makes you feel better, we'll do it Slim's way and tie him up along the gate. Then he can't buck you off."

Cuaifeach watched suspiciously as he had his head tied by a rope to one gate post and his off hind leg by a shorter rope to the other. He did not like it at all, he shifted uneasily.

"I'll give you a leg up," Jake offered.

But in doing so, he forgot that it was only a pony Andy was mounting, not a great big cowboy horse. The mighty shove he gave him was enough to send him, not into the saddle, but high above it and down the other side of the gate, where Andy ended up, flat on his back. Cuaifeach looked down at him, astonished.

"Sorry about that," Jake mumbled. "Come

again!"

"Without your help, if you please," said Andy.

"Just remember to sit down gently on him. Not like a ton of bricks, like you usually do."

"You're one to speak!" Andy exclaimed, offended. "Why do you think he bucked you off before?"

He climbed the gate and lowered himself into the saddle, with a touch as light as that of a butterfly. Cuaifeach did not stir. Andy turned to his brother with a triumphant smile.

"A ton of bricks, you said?"

"Okay, okay," Jake said impatiently, "now go forward."

"How can I go forward when he's all tied up?"

Jake quickly undid the ropes. Then Andy smacked and shoved and gave plenty of leg, but Cuaifeach did not move. He stood as if he was rooted to the ground. "Perhaps he believes he is still tied up?" Andy suggested.

"This pony," Jake said slowly, "is either the cutest or the most stupid animal I have ever come across."

He reached for his whip.

"No!" Andy cried in alarm. "I'd rather get him going myself. Let me have your spurs!"

But no effort, not even Jake's silver spurs, could induce Cuaifeach to take a single step forward or sideways or backwards. He just gave a quiver as if the spurs tickled him.

"I've had enough of this," Jake muttered. "Go on!" he roared, giving an almighty whack with the whip.

The pony leapt from standstill over the gate and ran away down the drive. Andy found himself once more prostrate in the puddle.

Wearily the brothers pursued the stallion but could not see him anywhere. They went up on to the road, from where they would be able to survey the surroundings.

"We'd better find him before anyone realises what's happened," Jake said. "I wouldn't like this to get around Connemara."

He had hardly said this, when Johnny Tass came whizzing round the bend in his car. The O'Briens tried to look casual, as if they were out for a pleasurable stroll in the rain, certainly not on the look-out for anything. Johnny pulled up next to them.

"Down the beach," he said and then added with a wink, before driving on: "Arkle wouldn't have run half as fast."

Cuaifeach was playing in the surf, running in and out of it with great gusto, against the wind that had now got up to gale force. When he discovered the brothers, he galloped off a little further along the vast beach, then looked back at them with a look of amusement on his face. "Come and get me," he seemed to say, "come and get me if you can, ho, ho."

The O'Briens looked helplessly at each other.

"What do we do?" Andy asked his brother.

Jake heaved a big sigh. "I'm darned if I know."

"What would Slim have done?"

"Oh, I can tell you that. He would have thrown a lasso around his neck, choked him until he blacked out, and then, while he was down, shown him who was boss."

"Can't we do that?"

Jake shook his head. "Slim wasn't always right," he said slowly.

"Slim was great!" Andy cried, outraged. "He knew everything, all the tricks..."

"Well some tricks that work in the Wild West may not work in Connemara," said Jake. "Try throwing a lasso in a force nine gale for a start. Even Slim couldn't have done that."

Andy thought grimly about this while Jake despondently watched the pony enjoying himself.

"Aren't you able to catch him?" they

suddenly heard a girl's light voice behind them.

Jake swivelled round. "Of course we are! He's only having his hooves washed. It's very good for them, salt water."

"He's my pony," the girl said softly.

"That explains a lot," Andy muttered.

"How did you get on?" Doreen asked, but even as she said it, she realised that it probably wasn't a very tactful question. The brothers' appearance, especially set against Cuaifeach's carefree behaviour, spoke for itself: they looked dirty and dishevelled and generally crestfallen. The one with the strangely shaped hat limped as he walked, and the other, shorter one had a bandaged hand in a sling made from a grubby spotted kerchief.

"We got on all right," said Andy, loath to give up the credit for this one small achievement.

"But we got off again pretty quickly," Jake added with a wry smile.

"Was he really that bad?" the girl asked anxiously.

Jake drew a deep breath. "I don't really think he's a bad pony," he said. "It just didn't work out like we had expected."

"We're not used to horses like him," Andy explained.

"No," Jake filled in. "We sure have a thing or two to learn about Connemara ponies."

❋❋❋

Christy was very quiet as he drove Doreen and Cuaifeach home. In the end the girl had had to wade out into the sea to catch her pony. He had only agreed to come when the O'Briens made themselves scarce, so there was obviously no point in leaving him with them for further instruction.

When they arrived at Inishnee, Christy did not get out but stayed behind the wheel, staring stonily at the daffodils in the Joyces' front garden, as if he expected them to provide the answer to whatever he was brooding over. Doreen waited. She had a pretty good idea what was on his mind.

"I'll still...er...have him broke for you," Christy said eventually. "At me own expense. I'm not one to go back on my word."

"But who is going to do it?" Doreen asked.

"I'll find someone," Christy promised airily. "You can rely on me, I'll stick to my end of the bargain."

"You mean as long as I stick to mine?" said the girl.

Christy turned to face her. His watery blue eyes expressed such grave concern that it almost made her laugh. "Will you?" he asked.

"Take him to the inspection, you mean? Oh, I suppose so, if it means that much to you."

Christy's eyes glittered like the sea in June. "You're a grand girleen," he said.

3

uite a few people like to attend the stallion inspection that takes place in Connemara every year at the end of May. It is of course a matter of interest to the breeders in the area to find out what young stallions will be available to them in years to come. Besides, the local people are curious to see who has a colt good enough to be presented for inspection and eager to witness the honour, as Christy put it, of those lucky few who will have their animal passed. Some tourists also will find their way to the event as well as the odd overseas buyer, always a popular figure.

Then there are the officials: stallion inspectors, a specially appointed vet, and the administrators of the Connemara Pony Breeders' Society. The latter go around to a number of venues to inspect and register youngstock: mares and geldings can be presented all over the region, but the two- and three-year-old stallions only in one place, at this time, Maam Cross. They are followed by a retinue of outsiders who all have a vested interest in the development of the Connemara pony: breeders from other parts of Ireland or even Britain, judges and other experts, all of whom make the annual inspection of youngstock a good excuse for an early summer outing to the West.

First on the scene this dull, overcast morning were the locals. They greeted each other as usual with comments on the weather, the one force that ruled the life of all of them on equal terms. "Depressing sort of day," said one man, "nice and mild," another. A third thought the day was "quite chilly", while a fourth pronounced it "very close". Some people, even, had different remarks for different people. To an onlooker this might have seemed confusing, but then, statements such as these were never meant to be accurate reports on the weather conditions but more an expression of your own frame of mind. And come to think of it, each person was right, in his own way. Your perception of the weather, like so many other things, depends entirely on your own outlook. There is something good and something bad to be said about every day.

By eleven-thirty, seven colts had arrived on the scene, and the spectators were walking around appraising them as they were paraded by their owners. A couple of ponies were regarded as certainties, having won important prizes as yearling colts in the shows of the previous summer. It was obvious that these had been pampered over the winter and stuffed with expensive supplementary feedstuffs: they were bursting with condition and as large as mature ponies. One was cream-coloured, a good fourteen-two. He belonged to a retired army major who had a stud near Tuam—not quite Connemara, but near enough, and with the benefit of the good grass in East Galway. The other was a rangy light grey who had won not only his class but also the Reserve Championship at the big show in Clifden. His owner was a plasterer from Oughterard who had produced a couple of good stallions before. The remaining four colts apart from Cuaifeach came from small farms in different parts of Connemara and showed a varying degree of roughness. Their chances were thought to be slim, but then, you never quite knew what the inspectors were looking for: it could be a rare bloodline, for example, in danger of dying out. Where Cuaifeach was concerned, people seemed to be keeping an open mind. For one thing, they had not seen him yet as he refused to come out of his trailer.

Christy was exhausted. Only the drive to Maam Cross had been an ordeal. They had hardly crossed the causeway from Inishnee, when he and Doreen heard a loud bang and stamping from the trailer behind the car. As he checked anxiously in his wing mirror, Christy was astonished to find himself staring straight into the big brown eyes of the stallion, who was supposed to have his head safely tied up inside the trailer. The long black mane was flying in the wind, remnants of his brand-new head-collar flapping round his head. He must have bust the head-collar and turned himself round to stick his head out of the gap at the back of the trailer. Now he was travelling back to front with his head turned right round so that he could see where he was going. Each time they passed a mare in a field, he sent out a resounding stallion cry that made not only every pony in the area, but also every motorist on the road turn his head.

So they had proceeded, Doreen going on about stopping to reload him the right way round, Christy arguing that it was a waste of time as he was bound to do the same thing over again.

A coach passed them, full of French students waving frantically at the stallion, who returned the compliment with yet another ear-splitting whinny. But he shut up for a while after they hit a large puddle where the road was flooded at Ballinahinch—it all but drenched him, and what Christy saw in the mirror looked remarkably like a drowned rat.

"After all the trouble I took grooming him!" Doreen wailed.

"Now you must leave everything to me," Christy instructed his grand-niece as they approached Maam Cross. "Presenting a stallion is a man's job. I'll have no interference—you keep out of the way."

So when they arrived Doreen limited her assistance to brushing the mud off the pony's face and mending the broken head-collar with a piece of blue baling-twine that she found in the car. It looked rather tatty, especially when compared to the major's brassy show bridle, but it couldn't be helped. Worse was the fact that Uncle Christy couldn't get him to unload. He pulled and heaved and cursed, but Cuaifeach only dug his heels in and stayed where he was, silent now in the cacophony of young colts calling out to one another. People had begun to gather around to watch and were contributing some gleeful advice.

"He wants a good shove from behind," one man hinted.

"Very well," Christy panted, "You get in there behind him and give him one. I won't, for sure!"

"Show him a bucket!" was another suggestion.

But there was no bucket at hand. Cuaifeach remained in the trailer.

"Where is that blasted girl?" Christy finally cried out in despair. "She was supposed to help."

Doreen appeared from behind the car. "You told me to keep away."

"Well just see if he'll come to you."

The girl went up and without any fuss at all led the stallion out of the trailer.

"Well I never," Christy said deprecatingly to the crowd, and then took himself off to the bar to restore his strength.

One person was staring at the colt with a look of tender pride in his eyes, like a father seeing his darling child about to win a major prize on school sports day. He was Marty MacDonagh, Cuaifeach's own breeder, who had come along after hearing a rumour that his former pet was going to be presented.

"Didn't he come on?" he mumbled, his voice thick with emotion. "Didn't he come on?"

"There's good growth in him," his friend Paddy Pat conceded.

At this point the inspectors arrived with their followers, a long row of gleaming smart cars, very unlike the mud-stained rusty bangers already lining the road. They trooped off in orderly ranks, most of the men wearing suits and ties, the women equally well-dressed, some stepping carefully to avoid getting mud on their shoes. That, of course, is a sure way of telling a stranger in Connemara, the residents being all resigned to having constantly dirty footwear.

To begin with, they wandered round viewing the colts, exchanging well-versed remarks, asking the odd question of the owners, who, flattered by the interest, happily obliged. One of the visitors was a tidy-looking man of slight build, with pale blue eyes behind steel-framed spectacles and sandy, short-cropped hair. He and a woman wearing a colourful silk scarf went up to Cuaifeach. They looked the pony over but did not seem too impressed.

"What have we here?" the man enquired.

"Cuaifeach," Doreen replied, more timid than usual.

"Speak English!" said the man. "I take it you know how to?"

"His name is Cuaifeach," said Marty who was standing next to her.

"Oh!" the man laughed dismissively. "These Irish names," he said to the woman, "they sound like something you've got stuck in your throat."

"What's his breeding?" the woman asked in a cultured English voice.

"He's out of Veronica," Marty said smugly, knowing full well the effect this piece of information would have on anyone who knew the slightest thing about Connemara ponies.

"Oh that one? I've heard about him," said the man and added to his companion: "You can see why they didn't let her breed again."

Doreen and Marty exchanged a glance of mute indignation.

"Makes you wonder, doesn't it?" the man went on. "That a mare like Veronica should have produced something like that. Makes you wonder if you can really trust the stud book in these parts."

They moved on. Marty was at a loss for words.

"Who is that fellow?" he blurted out at last. "How dare he come here and say things like that?"

"He's from the East," Paddy Pat informed him, as if that explained everything. "His name is Ovenpad."

"Ovenpad?" Marty repeated queryingly.

"Well, he's really Owen Paddy, but we call him Ovenpad. Because he's a great one for bolstering himself. See what I mean?" Paddy Pat added with a wink.

Marty did. So the man was one of these fellows who hung around in search of foreign customers. He would advise buyers not to deal directly with the Connemara men, "who were only out to cheat them", but leave all negotiations to himself, who would be only too happy to oblige. This meant adding a hefty sum to the asking price—an extra profit margin which, unbeknownst to the buyer, would go straight into the negotiator's pocket. Funny how those foreigners didn't see further than their noses.

"I wouldn't worry about anything Ovenpad says," Paddy Pat went on. "He's forever knocking ponies just to get the prices down."

"That's easy for you to say," Marty retorted. "You haven't been accused of fiddling the stud book."

Doreen heard none of this. She had taken Cuaifeach aside and was busy scratching his midge bites. The midges were bad in May.

The inspection started. With a measuring-stick and note-books the committee dealt with the colts one by one. Each owner was told to trot his pony up and down on the road to Maam. Some of the colts played up, excited and distracted by all the attention. Traffic had to be held up, as each animal's movement was studied, from behind and from the front, over and over. Anything other than absolute straightness led to elimination. Their height was measured, foaling papers examined, notes taken.

In due course they came to Cuaifeach. He was standing quietly, waiting his turn, intimidated perhaps, by the presence of so many other colts. Also helpful was the fact that Christy had not emerged from the bar in time. He was still nursing his bruised ego with measures of Irish whiskey so it was Doreen who had to take care of the pony. One inspector asked for his blue foal certificate and glanced at it briefly.

"So this is the famous Cuaifeach," he said.

The colt nodded his head up and down affirmatively.

"Or should I say infamous?"

Cuaifeach shook his head vigorously from side to side.

"At least he has a sense of humour," said another committee member.

Throughout the inspection the colt behaved impeccably. He stood up proudly, inviting them all to admire him, and trotted smartly up and down, casting glances in the direction of the committee, as if he wanted to check that they weren't missing anything. The inspectors discreetly communicated their views between them:

"They say he has a filthy temperament. We do have to take that into account as well."

"Filthy temperament? When did you ever see a stallion handled by a young girl? And by God, he is the most obedient of the lot of them."

"Pity about the colour. Bay always makes them look more plain."

"At three years of age I like to see them higher in the withers. And the hind quarters could be stronger."

"Plenty of bone, though."

"It is, of course, all we have after Veronica. All we're likely to have, by the looks of it."

Then there was only one colt left to inspect. He belonged to two cousins, Tom Samuel and

Joe Will, so called after their respective fathers, Samuel and Will. They lived in a small cottage way up in the Bens, where they scraped a meagre living from sheep-farming and whatever else they could think of. They had a long-standing reputation of being none too straight: one of them had been in prison for making poteen, illegal homebrew. Their pony was as scruffy and ill-kempt as the cousins themselves. It had the big blown-up belly and matt shaggy coat that are sure signs of advanced worm infestation, and its growth had been severely stunted by lack of nutrition.

To people who did not know the cousins it was hard to fathom why they had taken the trouble of bringing him at all, it was so obvious that he would not be passed. But Tom Samuel and Joe Will were inveterate chancers, who, rather than size up their odds, lived by the principle that, if you kept trying, circumstances would occasionally work out in your favour. And in this they weren't always wrong. People used to say they were far luckier than they deserved.

However, no good fortune in the world could have turned the tables in favour of this colt. To the inspectors he was not really worth bothering with, but since everyone had to be given a fair chance, they had to go through the procedure of inspecting it. There was some initial confusion when the inspector from the Department went up to the owners with his note-book. He was new to the job and had never come across the cousins before.

"Can you give me the name of the owner?" he said to Joe Will with a disparaging glance at the poor animal.

"Joe Will!" Joe Will blurted out in his loud, abrupt manner.

"Is that you?" said the inspector turning to Tom Samuel, who was holding the pony.

"I'm Tom Samuel," said Tom Samuel.

"Well where is he then?" the inspector demanded impatiently.

"Who?" Tom Samuel asked.

"This...Joe, whoever he is, who will give me the name of the owner."

"I'm Joe," said Joe.

"For God's sake, why didn't you say so?" the inspector snapped. "Now will you give me the name?"

"Joe Will," said Joe Will.

From the look of despair on the inspector's face, it seemed that the whole thing would have started again from the beginning, if it hadn't been for one of the other inspectors coming to the rescue of his colleague, telling him the man's name was Joe Will.

"Where there's a Will, there's a way," said Seamus Lee.

The inspection proceeded. The colt was measured at thirteen-one.

"He is rather small," one inspector told the cousins, as if they couldn't see that for themselves.

"We'll only run him with our own mares," Tom Samuel reassured him. "We needn't use him for any of the others."

"That doesn't make any difference," the inspector admonished him. "If he isn't good enough to breed from, he isn't good enough for anyone."

"It would only be two or three," Joe Will persisted. He was eating crisps from a bag as he talked, and his whole face was contorted, as he was trying to get the molars of his upper right to meet those of his lower left—they were the only teeth he had left.

Their work completed, the inspection committee withdrew for a brief conference.

"I take it we can eliminate the last one," said the man from the Department.

"To tell you the truth," said one of the other inspectors in a confidential tone suggesting that this was not his normal practice, "I'd be loath to register anything coming from those two even if it had the looks of a champion. We could never trust their papers to be correct, and it would play havoc with the stud book."

The spectators waited eagerly to hear their verdict as the committee returned. And there was a sensation in store for them: the major's cream-coloured favourite had been turned down. It had shown a slight dish on the off fore, and was considered too long in the body.

"Just what I thought!" Johnny Tass exclaimed proudly. "I said to meself, that one looks more like Mrs Moran's Pekinese than a Connemara pony!"

As expected, the light grey colt from Oughterard passed with flying colours. Another surprise was the approval of a sturdy steel-grey pony from the stony lands of South Connemara. Its owner was a poor smallholder, who had never had much success with his ponies, though his family had bred them for generations. He was so delighted he could hardly believe it was true. And then the inspectors delivered the final sensation: the third and last pony to be approved as a breeding stallion was Cuaifeach.

Marty was over the moon. Forgetting that

she was just a girl, he slapped Doreen's back, almost winding her. "Congratulations!" he cried. "Oh I haven't been so pleased since... since Veronica won in Dublin! You must be delighted, too! This must be the happiest day of your life!"

"It is," Doreen smiled, her eyes shining. "I thought I didn't care, but I really am pleased, so I am."

Soon she was surrounded by well-wishers, amongst them her Uncle Christy, who was delirious with joy.

"Well done, girl!" he shouted, magnanimous in his moment of triumph. "Well done! It's all thanks to you!"

"It's all thanks to Cuaifeach," the girl said, looking affectionately at the colt who was prancing around, showing off to everyone. "Do you know, I think he really wanted to be passed, that's why he behaved so well. Oh, he's so clever!"

As the men went off to celebrate, an American visitor approached Doreen. He looked approvingly at the stallion and asked: "How much do you want for him?"

"He's not for sale," Doreen replied, smiling as Cuaifeach bent forward to sniff the American's after-shave and then quickly withdrew with a shudder.

"Come on now," said the man equably, "I'll give you a good price for him."

"I'm not selling him," the girl explained. "Not for all the money in the world."

"Hey," the American said, a note of impatience creeping into his voice, "I wanna speak to your parents. They will know better than to reject an offer like mine."

"It's nothing to do with my parents," Doreen declared. "He's my pony and I'm not selling him."

The American left her in some vexation. A little later a well-dressed, respectable-looking man came up to him.

"My name is Ryan," he said courteously, holding out his hand to him. "Owen Paddy Ryan. Are you really interested in that colt?"

"I sure am," replied the American, who had never heard of Ovenpad and took the man to be just a friendly stranger. "I'm a breeder of Connemaras myself," he went on, "and we're having terrible problems back home with albino foals. I've been told the only safe bet is to get a bay stallion, the bay colour breaks the albino gene. But a good bay is not easily come by. And now that stupid child refuses to sell hers."

Owen Paddy Ryan gave him a conspiratorial smile. "In Connemara all ponies are for sale. These people can't afford otherwise. But they are cute. You have to know how to deal with them."

"Well would you have a word with that girl and her parents on my behalf? I sure didn't get anywhere with her."

"I'll be delighted," Ovenpad said, meaning every word. "But perhaps you should give me some indication of the sort of money you're prepared to pay for him."

"I'd go as far as five thousand," said the American. "That's how much he'd be worth to me."

"Pounds?" the helpful stranger asked.

"Dollars. Oh well then, pounds," the American corrected himself when he saw the look of hesitation on the other man's face. "That would keep the whole family going for a year, wouldn't it? They couldn't turn down an offer like that?"

"Leave it to me," said Owen Paddy Ryan. "I'll do what I can for you."

He still sounded slightly doubtful.

"Listen," the American resumed, "if you can get them to settle for a little less, I'm quite happy for you to keep the balance. My five

thousand are on the table. I want that pony.
But you save whatever you can for your
pocket."

Ovenpad amiably shook his hand. This was
the sort of thing he liked to hear. It was always
nice, tidy somehow, to have it condoned. He
left the American with a conspiratorial wink.

"Give me half an hour," he said.

In the bar Christy was the object of much
hand-shaking and back-slapping. Over and
over again he told the story of his efforts to
get Doreen to agree to bring the pony to the
inspection. Owen Paddy Ryan listened carefully
and then joined the crowd around him.

"He really is a beautiful colt," he said to
Christy, who had never seen him before. "You
must be very proud of him."

Marty, hearing this behind him, choked and
spluttered over his beer. "Did you hear that?"
he hissed to Paddy Pat next to him. "An hour
ago he spoke as if the pony wasn't worth the
bit of leather he had on his head!"

"I'm pleased for the girl's sake," Christy
replied. "The honour is well deserved. She done
him well, and a lot of hard work it's taken her."

"I suppose he'll be sold now?" the stranger
suggested. "He'll be worth a lot of money."

"Sold? Never! The colt means the earth to

her. He's the only joy she has. God knows, things are hard enough for her at home."

"I hear her mother is worse again," Johnny Tass prompted him, as always on the lookout for fresh information.

Christy shook his head gravely. "I don't know where it's going to end. It's a great worry to all of us. She really ought to have specialist treatment, but you know how long the waiting lists are."

A cunning glint had lit in Owen Paddy's eye. "Really?" he said. "The girl's mother is ill? What's wrong with her?"

"It's something I don't care to discuss," Christy replied curtly. He had forgotten the stranger in their midst and resented the interest he was taking in matters that did not concern him.

"Women's trouble?" the man ventured.

The mention of those words in public made Christy so embarrassed that he stared grimly into his stout and did not utter another word for several minutes.

Owen Paddy Ryan, taking his silence for confirmation, slipped out of the bar and went to seek out Doreen. She had climbed a grass bank to let Cuaifeach graze and the stallion was munching away, quiet and contented, as if fresh succulent grass was all he could ever ask from life. When the stranger came up, she received him suspiciously, remembering only too well the last time he had accosted her. But the man's attitude had completely changed. He smiled kindly and held out a hand to pat the colt, although he soon pulled it back, when Cuaifeach snatched at him.

"I was wrong about him," he said meekly. "To be honest, I don't know the first thing about Connemara ponies. Can't even tell a good one when it's staring me in the face."

He gave an apologetic little laugh.

Doreen said nothing.

"So what are you going to do with him now?" the man chatted on. "Surely a girl like you couldn't manage a breeding stallion?"

"I'll have him gelded," Doreen told him.

"But that's crazy!" the man exclaimed. "You have no right to do that now that he's been approved. If that was your intention, you shouldn't have brought him here in the first place. Don't you see, he's taken the slot from one of the others. You can't have him gelded!"

"I can," said Doreen determinedly. "He's my pony, I can do exactly as I please with him."

"Well look at it this way," the man resumed after a little pause. "It would be bad economy.

You could sell this one and buy yourself a smart gelding for half—less than half—the money. That would leave you with a nice little nest-egg, wouldn't it?"

"I'm not interested in money," said the girl.

There was another pause. Then the man said slowly: "I hear your Mam isn't too well."

Doreen spun round to face him. "Who told you that?"

He ignored her question. "It just occurred to me, when I heard it, that it's strange that a child can be so selfish. So unconcerned about her own mother."

"What's all this to do with you?" Doreen asked, now obviously distressed.

The man was looking out over the lake in front of him, biding his time, as it were, while Doreen became increasingly uneasy. Then he launched his attack:

"You say you're not interested in money. Are you really so dim that you don't realise your mother's health is all a matter of money? She needs to see a good doctor, a specialist. But private doctors cost money, money she hasn't got. Here you are with a pony that could be worth as much as—as much as two thousand pounds. And you won't sell him! Well you'll remember that one day when your Mam is no longer around."

Doreen's face had gone very white. Her gaze was fixed on Cuaifeach's hind pasterns.

"Who are you?" she asked in a low trembling voice. "Who sent you to tell me this?"

The man looked her up and down, as if he was making an assessment. Then he said: "My name is Ryan. I'll give you two thousand pounds for your pony. You have until eleven o'clock tomorrow morning to make up your mind. I'll be around then to collect him, assuming you've come to your senses."

Doreen did not see him go. She had her face buried in Cuaifeach's thick mane and her shoulders were shaking with the effort of holding back her tears.

So much for the happiest day of her life!

The Price of Love

4

trailer did collect Cuaifeach the following day. But it wasn't Owen Paddy Ryan's trailer, and the stallion was loaded with much good cheer and laughter. Then Doreen climbed in next to the driver of the car and she smiled and waved as they departed. She thought to herself, never did I know such sadness...and such gladness...and all in such a short space of time!

There hadn't been much sleep for her the previous night. She had lain in her bed, tossing and turning as Mr Ryan's words tossed and turned in her head. More than anything she wanted to get away from them, sink into a deep oblivious slumber, but it was the very truth of those words that kept her awake, the knowledge that there was no escape from them: she was to lose one, if not both, of those two beings she loved most in the world.

It had not occurred to her before that her mother's illness might be serious, even life-threatening. She and Tom had grown to accept the fact that their mother was unwell as just one aspect of the deplorable change that had come over their family since the older children left and their father went to work in England. It was a great pity, and they felt sorry for her, but for them it was no worse than missing their Dad. At least she was still there—the only one of the big family who was still with them—and that was what mattered most. If they were to lose her too...Oh no, Doreen thought desperately, she mustn't die! If anything at all could be done to save her, it had to be done.

Even if it meant parting from her beloved pony...

Too restless to stay in bed, Doreen went over to the open window. It was a warm and humid night, wafts of damp grass and seaweed came drifting into the room. Daybreak wasn't far away, there was a shimmer of red just above the horizon and streaks of orange licked the edges of the great black mass of the sea. The stillness of the night was beginning to break up: the early cry of a gull, seals barking on distant rocks, a small rabbit scuttling past the house on its way to the potato garden. Doreen took all of this in with a feeling that it would be etched on her mind for ever. For this was the moment when she finally made her decision. The decision she had tried in vain to escape from.

She would sell Cuaifeach. Let him go, not knowing where he would end up, how he would be treated, whether he would ever be loved by anyone again. From now on she would wake up in the morning without a hungry stallion waiting for her to bring his breakfast. There would be no shed to clean out, no hay or straw to carry across the field. Summer had come, but there would be none of the happy outings she had promised her pony, no treks, no playing in the sea.

What would he get instead?

Oh, there was no point tormenting herself with these thoughts, when she knew there was no other solution! Now her decision was made and that was all there was to it.

A strange kind of peace came over her, as sometimes happens when you are made to face the worst and act upon it. The sadness was as profound, the pain as searing, but at least she was no longer struggling against them. With this feeling akin to relief Doreen got back into bed and curled up, suddenly very tired. Before long she had drifted into a shallow sleep.

She dreamt that she heard a car approaching the cottage. Then she woke with a start, realising she wasn't dreaming at all. The room was still dim, so she could only have been asleep for a few minutes. It's Mr Ryan, she thought drowsily; he's come for Cuaifeach. But why so early? He said eleven o'clock. Wasn't he going to let her have even those few hours to say goodbye to her stallion?

Then it came to her that no one in his right mind would come to buy a pony in the small hours of the morning. No one came at all at that time, unless...unless he was up to no good. Was Mr Ryan going to steal Cuaifeach, take him away without paying for him? She tiptoed to the window and looked out. A van, a bright red van, was being parked in front of the cottage. But there was no horse-trailer attached to it. Cuaifeach was safe, at least for the moment.

So what was going on? Doreen thought of the front door, as usual left unlocked. "If I had anything worth stealing," her mother used to say, "and had to lock my door at night, that's when I'd start worrying."

Doreen decided to go and wake Tom, who slept in the room across the landing. As the family grew, their father had converted the loft into two small bedrooms with sloping ceilings, and the two remaining children now occupied one each—a luxury the older children wouldn't have dreamt of. When she passed the top of the stairs, she heard the front door open. Heavy boots walked across the floor of the kitchen, and then the light was switched on. With her heart in her mouth, Doreen peeped down at the man who had entered the cottage. The next moment she came tumbling down the steep staircase, flung herself in his arms and clung to him as if she feared that he would otherwise turn round and walk out again. Tears were running down her cheeks but they were tears of joy, a joy so intense that for a moment it blotted out her despair.

"Dad!" she cried. "Oh Dad, you came back!"

He was just as she remembered him, big and strong and smelling nicely of sawdust and tobacco. Only his clothes were new, and his hair looked tidier than it used to. He laughed and hugged her.

"Of course I came back," he said. "Didn't you think I would?"

It was as if the whole world had returned to

normality in an instant. Doreen put the kettle on, while he sat down and took off his boots, chatting about his long journey. He had driven all the way from London, docked at Rosslare at midnight and driven on through the night.

"Don't wake the others," he warned her. "They be better off sleeping."

"Why didn't you let us know you were coming?" Doreen asked him.

"Well I decided on the spur of the moment," he replied, and then he fell silent, as if he had been reminded of something worrisome. "I had a letter from the doctor in Roundstone," he explained. "About Mam."

"Oh..." Now Doreen, too, remembered, and her anxiety returned even stronger than before.

"I never knew it was so bad with her," her father went on gravely. "She never let on in her letters."

"No," Doreen said despondently. "She didn't want to worry you."

"Well I wish someone had let me know," her father stated. "I would have been back sooner."

"I didn't realise," Doreen said, "how serious it was. Mam never wanted to talk about it. But now she'll get well again, Dad, we'll take her to the best doctor in Galway, and you needn't worry about the money, because I..." Her voice faltered.

"What are you on about?" her father asked, confused.

Doreen drew a deep breath. "I'm selling Cuaifeach," she said.

"Selling him? Why? I thought you liked that pony."

"Oh I do, Dad, I love him more than I ever did, but I couldn't keep him, not with Mam sick and needing the money to get well. If we lost her, how could I ever forgive myself?"

A deep furrow had appeared between her father's eyebrows. It was, she recalled, a sure sign that he was angry. But when he spoke his voice was gentle.

"Come here," he said. "Whoever put this nonsense into your head?"

"But I do want her to get well," Doreen declared. "More than anything, more even than I would love to keep Cuaifeach."

"Who told you she needed money for a doctor?" her father asked sternly.

"A man called Mr Ryan. He is not from around here. And he's offered me two thousand pounds for Cuaifeach. That will be enough, won't it, Dad, to get Mam well again?"

Her father looked as though a mighty thundercloud had settled over his head. "Never in my life have I heard anything so rotten," he said hoarsely. "Where can I find this man?"

"He's coming today, at eleven, to collect Cuaifeach." As she said it, tears rose in her eyes.

"He'll be collecting a good thrashing from me," her father muttered. "To deceive a child...you'd think there's no shame left in this world."

Deceive a child, he had said. Deceive a child? What did he mean? Doreen battled with the conclusion beginning to form in her mind, defending herself against the hope it held out, a hope that might, after all, turn out to be false. But she had to know, had to ask him. In a small voice she said: "Do you mean I don't have to sell him?"

Her father held out his hand and pulled her onto his lap, as he used to do when she was little. "My girleen," he said tenderly, "things would have to be very bad indeed for us to accept such a sacrifice from you. God grant they never will be. You hold on to your pony. He's yours by right. And that's what you should say to anyone who tries to tell you otherwise."

But there was no delight written on the girl's face. She looked bewildered, as if she didn't quite believe him. Perhaps this is what happens, her father thought sadly, when you stay away too long. Your children lose their trust in you.

"Surely you're pleased to hear that?" he said.

Doreen slid off his lap. "What about Mam?" she asked, as if she doubted his concern for her.

"I'll tell you now," her father began, "what the doctor told me in his letter. He is a very good doctor, you know, to go to such trouble. And he doesn't cost us a penny."

"Did he say what's wrong with her?"

Her father nodded. "He did. What she suffers from is depression."

"But that's no illness," Doreen objected. "She had an operation...for gall-stones...that's when it all started."

Her father replied that, apparently, it could happen that way. If your system was weakened for some such reason, the depression could get a hold of you. There were two kinds, the doctor had explained, one that came for no good reason, eating you from inside, as it were— that was the worst kind, because it was difficult to cure. Then there was the other kind, which had a real cause, and that was more like a grief that had gone out of control. A grief that took you over so that you couldn't live or behave normally. That was the kind Doreen's mother suffered from.

The girl silently took all this in. So her mother was not really sick, but grieving. Grieving for what? It was a long time since they had a bereavement. But looking back, it made sense. She thought of her mother at their Christmas dinner, picking listlessly at her plateful of the turkey that she and Tom had had to beg her to get out of bed to prepare. Such a picture of misery she had been, on the day that should have been the happiest of the year!

"But this kind," her father continued, "can be treated and cured. And not by expensive doctors, as your Mr Ryan would have it, but rather, the doctor says, by the patient's own family. All we have to do is find the cause and do something about it."

Doreen remembered a night just before Christmas. Eileen Ridge had come up with a Christmas parcel from their father, brought over by Eileen's husband who also worked in London but who, unlike their Dad, had come back to spend Christmas with his family. With her was Mary Tass, Johnny's wife, who went under the same nickname as her husband. She was certainly as fond of gossip as he was—but she lacked his kindly nature. A tall, thin woman with a pointed nose and thin lips, she seemed to have meanness stamped all over her. Mam, glad of the company, had received them with cups of tea and a taste of the Christmas cake.

"Isn't it a shame now, to be cutting the cake early?" Eileen had said.

"Oh well, I have no one to save it for," Mam replied with a smile.

"So it's true then, that Sean isn't coming back?" Mary Tass put in, a touch of triumph in her voice.

"He couldn't get the time off," Mam said hurriedly, as if she was anxious to defend her husband. "It wasn't worth it for just a couple of days...I mean, the ticket is dear enough."

"Of course," said Eileen Ridge, who was a kind soul and often showed her agreement by repeating what the other person had just said. "The ticket is dear enough, so it is."

Doreen looked at her father, who was busy rolling a cigarette. He lit it and puffed reflectively. Then he said: "The doctor thinks it's the loss of the family that got her down. It's not so long ago that the cottage was crawling with kids. Those were the days when your Mam was happy. And a good mother she was to ye all."

"She was," Doreen agreed. "I remember it well."

"And then suddenly one day, they were gone...scattered across the world..."

"She still has Tom and me!" Doreen interrupted. "Or perhaps we don't count?"

"Of course you count," her father said reassuringly. "But I suppose she thinks of the others, how quick they were to flee the nest, and then she sees the two of you as being next in turn. To her it's probably just a matter of time."

"I'll never leave Connemara," Doreen said doggedly.

Her father gave a little laugh. "They all say that to start with. Didn't I say so myself, until I was forty-six years old?"

"I don't believe any mother around here goes down with the depression just because her kids leave home," Doreen said slowly. "They know it's the only way if the children are to have a chance in life. Even Mam thinks so, she says she'd rather see us do well abroad than go to seed back home."

"It's one thing what a person says..." her father began.

"No!" Doreen interrupted him again. "It

wasn't the kids going what upset her. It wasn't that at all."

Her father gave her a sharp look. "What makes you say that?"

Doreen did not reply. The memory of Mary Tass's shrill, grinding voice was coming back to her: "If you ask me," she had said to Mam, who hadn't asked her at all, "you'll be lucky ever to see him again. You know what they say, once gone, gone forever. You won't be the first one."

"He'll be back in the summer," Mam had replied, again in that eager voice that seemed to suggest that she was desperate for the others to believe her. "And then he'll be back for good. That's what we've agreed on."

Mary Tass gave a sneering little laugh. "I can only say one thing. Connemara men are lucky to have unemployment to blame. Off they go, without a thought for the wives and children they leave behind. Just look at them— Kitty Keane, Aine Folan, Carmel Nee...all waiting and praying for husbands that will never show their face in Connemara again, except possibly to be buried. God knows what they get up to over there—but it must be something pleasurable, or they wouldn't have stayed away."

"What makes you say that?" her father repeated.

"I think she's been missing you," Doreen burst out. "She thought you had left her altogether. That the work was only an excuse."

Her father looked distinctly uncomfortable. "The rubbish coming out of you today," he said, shaking his head. "I've never heard the like of it."

"It was after Mary Tass told her..." Doreen started.

"She should have known better than listen to gossip!" her father boomed. "Mary Tass of all people, God save us all!"

He stabbed out his cigarette as if he wanted to hurt it.

"Oh well," he said then, "if that's what people have been telling her, it will be an easy enough matter to prove them wrong."

But Doreen wasn't satisfied. Now that she saw the connection, she was angry with her father for having put them to all this pain. How vulnerable they had all become, herself not least, because he had left them. What if he hadn't turned up at this very moment? Then she would have gone ahead and sold Cuaifeach—and all for no good reason.

"Oh Dad!" she cried. "Why did you have to

go to England? If only you had stayed, none of this would have happened!"

"Well I'm back now, anyways," her father said, an apologetic note in his voice revealing that he was not going to argue the point.

"Why did you go?" Doreen persisted.

Her father was silent for a while. "It's hard on a man," he said gruffly. "To be in your best years...to want to work and work hard...to know you have a skill and no call for it...see your family want for things and not be able to provide them...It seemed to me that the best I could do for myself...for ye all...was to go to where the work was. The work and the money."

At that point the bedroom door opened, and Doreen's mother appeared, wearing the blue candlewick dressing-gown that was all she ever wore nowadays. She stood there for a moment, blinking towards the light, still dazed by the sleeping pills the doctor had prescribed for her. She stared incredulously at her husband, but somewhere, deep in her eye, a light was beginning to shimmer. When she spoke, her words echoed those of her daughter.

"Sean," she said. "Sean. You came back."

A little later, Doreen slipped upstairs to bed. Her Mam and Dad did not notice.

❉❉❉

Christy was in for a surprise that morning, when he arrived at Inishnee and found his nephew Sean Joyce, not only at home but in the process of upbraiding the stranger who had appeared the day before at Maam Cross. The latter was doing his best to placate him, mumbling sheepish apologies to the effect of "having misread the situation", not wanting to "distress the young girl" and thinking he was "doing them all a good turn". Sean Joyce was not convinced, and neither, it seemed, was the man's own conscience, for when the other man, much bigger and stronger than himself, took a step in his direction, he flinched and quickly stumbled backwards.

"Don't you worry," Sean Joyce snarled at him, "I wouldn't like to waste my fists on scum like you. But if you don't pack yerself off this minute, I'll be sorely tempted."

At this the man retreated hurriedly to his car and proceeded to reverse the trailer nervously into the drive, with the result that one wheel got stuck in a deep rut. To get it out, he pressed the accelerator furiously, mud spurting from under his front wheels, but the trailer did not move. Christy and Sean watched calmly, until the man emerged looking rather like a dog with its tail between its legs. Without a word the two men acted: unhitched the trailer, turned it round manually, waited for the man to turn his car and then hitched up the trailer again. As he drove off, his hand stuck out the window, waving feebly by way of thanks. Sean Joyce, in reply, spat on the ground.

Christy was appalled when he heard what the man had been up to.

"Didn't I know that there was something wrong!" he exclaimed. "The girl didn't have a word to say for herself as we drove back from Maam Cross."

But whereas Sean Joyce was most incensed by the man's unscrupulous behaviour, it was the near loss of Cuaifeach that upset Christy.

"To think that we might have been without him," he moaned. "Dear God, that would have been a right disaster!"

It turned out that he had come to ask permission to have his last remaining old mare covered by Doreen's stallion.

"You have to ask the girl about that," said Sean. "It's her pony."

Christy sighed. That was exactly what he did not want to do.

They went into the cottage, where Roisin Joyce laid on tea for them. She was wearing a pretty summer dress and had washed her hair that morning. Christy remarked how pretty she looked, before turning to Doreen with his request. And just as he had feared, the girl was non-committal, said she'd think about it.

"But it has to be now," Christy insisted, "or the foal will be born too late in the season. Only early foals have a chance in the shows."

Doreen remained aloof. And Christy had to resort to what he had sworn he would not do: plead with her.

"It's not much to ask," he heard himself whining. "Just one foal, to have something left after him. After that I don't care what you do with him."

"Leave the girleen alone," said Sean. "She's been under enough pressure lately."

Christy fell into a gloomy silence. Sean obviously did not understand how much this meant to him personally. He was beginning to regret having boasted to everyone in the bar at Maam Cross that his Molly would be the first, probably the only mare ever to carry a foal by Cuaifeach. The statement had met with some derision.

"That mare has been barren for years," someone had said contemptuously.

"Of course she has," was Christy's riposte.

"Because I haven't given her the horse. There wasn't one good enough for her, that's why."

"Did she ever breed?" asked one of the younger men.

"Did she ever breed?" Christy repeated indignantly. "Fourteen foals she bore me, one each year, until..."

"Until she was well past it," another man filled in. "Come on, Christy, it wouldn't be fair on the old lady. Not on the horse either. You wouldn't marry off a young lad to an old grandmother."

The men laughed. Christy gritted his teeth, while his resolve strengthened. He was going to show them all. When his foal won its class in Clifden next summer...There would be no laughing then.

Seeing him so morose made Doreen take pity on him. She was fond of her grand-uncle, and now that her own problems had vanished so miraculously, she did not want to see anyone else unhappy. On the other hand, she didn't really want to part from Cuaifeach for any length of time.

"How long would you have to keep him?" she enquired reluctantly.

Hope was instantly rekindled in Christy's heart. "Three weeks at the most."

"Why so long?" the girl asked. "I thought it could be over and done with in a few minutes."

Christy embarked on a lengthy explanation. An old mare, being less fertile, was best left running with a stallion. And for two weeks out of the three, she wouldn't want to know him, she would kick and bite him and chase him away, as was the way with mares. Then suddenly, one day, she would wake up to the fact that he was the answer to her prayers and this blessed condition would last for up to a week. That was when mating would take place. After that you had to wait and see whether the mare came back into season. If she didn't, it meant most likely that she was in foal. But if she did come round again, the stallion would have to be brought back for another session.

Doreen said she thought it would be better to wait until Molly was well and truly in season and bring Cuaifeach over then. She didn't want him to be kicked and bitten.

"Well now," said Christy, stung again by the scornful words spoken at Maam Cross, "she doesn't come on as readily these days. After all, it's years since she saw a horse. It will take the steady company of one to get her going once more."

"What if it doesn't work?" Doreen said

dubiously.

"Of course it will work!" Christy cried. "There's not a mare the length and breadth of Ireland could resist your Cuaifeach!"

That finally clinched it.

❋❋❋

When her young suitor arrived, Molly the old grandmother was enjoying an afternoon nap in the field behind Christy's cottage. It had taken him the better part of the morning to get her into the enclosed space—normally she ran with the large wild herd out on the sand-dunes at Dunloughan. There had been no question of catching her—she had long since got out of such civilised habits. Driving her hadn't worked either, but he had succeeded, with the help of his sheep dog, in getting the whole herd down to a spot close to his field. Then he had opened up the stone wall in a suitable place and rattled some beef nuts in a black bucket—a sound that he knew from the past attracted Molly like flies to a lump of sugar. The only thing was that it had the same effect on some of the other mares. Christy had found himself with no less than nine ponies crowding the small field, trampling the juicy grass that was to feed the bridal couple in the weeks to come. He had to go and get help to chase them out while keeping Molly in, which had not been too difficult once she discovered that the grass in the field was sweeter than that outside. That task accomplished, Christy had lost no time in getting in behind the wheel and driving over to Inishnee.

Doreen stared in dismay at the dozing mare, at the coarse head drooping heavily down towards the big knees, at the front hooves turned out like the feet of a ballet dancer. The eyes were closed, the tufty ears at half-mast. Long white hairs were growing from the muzzle. The girl looked at the long hollow back, the loose low belly underneath it and she said to herself, poor thing, she can't help being old. Doreen loved all ponies; to her each one possessed its own special beauty. Yet she found herself regretting, for Cuaifeach's sake, that this one, his first and last girl-friend, wasn't just a shade more attractive.

"She's a grand mare," Christy said proudly, as Doreen led her excited pony up to the gate. "You couldn't have picked him a better one."

The stallion, amazingly, seemed to share this view, for he took one glance at the grey old lady and then whickered joyfully, as if congratulating himself on having managed to locate such a gorgeous creature. Molly, woken up by the sound, laid her ears back in annoyance at being disturbed but otherwise did not stir. Cuaifeach took a brisk gallop up to introduce himself as her gift from heaven. Molly's response was to bare lazily a set of very long, very yellow teeth.

"She doesn't seem too keen," Doreen observed.

"Give her time," Christy said, "give her time. In this game you have to be patient."

Patience, however, did not fit in with Cuaifeach's idea of courtship. He was progressing rapidly from sniffing the mare here and there, wherever he was out of reach of her formidable yellow teeth, to lustily licking her flanks.

"He's a real gentleman," Christy said approvingly. "He knows that a little coaxing goes a long way."

But Molly was not so easily wooed. She turned round and showed him her behind, a gesture as rude between horses as it is between humans. Poor Cuaifeach, innocent as he was, mistook the insult for an invitation and quickly mounted her. This provoked a vicious attack from the old mare, who swivelled round, set upon him with her front hooves and then chased him down to the opposite end of the field. There the youngster lingered, bewildered, while Molly settled down to graze, still with her ears glued back in an unmistakably hostile position.

"There's life in her yet," Christy said contentedly, and then he added: "Better leave them to it. Who would want spectators at a time like this?"

"Are you sure these walls are high enough?" Doreen asked anxiously as they left.

"He won't go anywhere," Christy reassured her. "Why would he, when he has Molly at hand?"

5

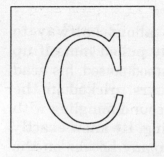uaifeach, give him his due, persevered for almost two weeks in relentless courtship of the reluctant Molly. But he got nothing for his trouble except kicks and bites, and in the end he concluded that his valiant romantic efforts were falling on stony ground.

It was a lovely morning in early June that he jumped the gate out of the field at Ballyconneely and took to the road in the direction of Inishnee. Molly watched him go without a flicker of regret. He strolled along in a leisurely way, stopping now and then to sample the wild flowers of the verge: harebells and cow-parsley, buttercups and St John's Wort and a budding foxglove, which, however, he soon spat out again.

Foreign motorists slammed on the brakes in

alarm when they saw him, while the locals, unconcerned, from a distance took him to be one of the mares from Dunloughan, who occasionally strayed onto the road. It was probably as well that, this morning, there were no mares on the road.

The stallion had got about halfway to Murvey when he suddenly pulled himself up in an attentive stance: he stood poised, his head turned to the side, his ears pricked in the direction of a distant dull sound mingling with the lark-song of the morning. He knew exactly what it was: the beat of many hooves on the road. Many hooves, on their way towards him.

❈❈❈

Some time in April, about the time of the Easter eggs, Andy O'Brien had hatched what he thought was a splendid idea. It had taken some persuasion to get Jake to go along with the project, but now it was in full swing: The O'Briens' Trekking Centre at Murvey, offering day-long rides to the guests of some expensive hotels in the Clifden area. In a flashy leaflet, American-style, tourists were promised "the experience of a life-time": riding along deserted country roads, galloping on coral beaches,

admiring the spectacular views of Connemara
from the vantage point of hilltops too rough
for human feet to tread. The brothers had spent
many days exploring the environs, unearthing
old tracks, cutting back undergrowth, reinforc-
ing boggy stretches with stone. On sunny days,
like this one, the trek followed the road to
Mannin Beach, where horses and riders would
cavort in the sea, jump stone walls specially
erected for the purpose and generally tear
around.

Five customers had turned up that morning,
which to Jake's mind meant two hundred and
fifty pounds, money they sorely needed, having
spent far too much buying horses. The trekkers
were all from continental Europe. The O'Briens
never kept track of nationalities, a foreigner
was a foreigner as far as they were concerned,
and any strange-sounding name was translated
into the most similar English version that they
could pronounce. Jake introduced the trekkers
to each other: there were Victor and Francesca,
Sophie and Marie, and Philip. Victor was a
grey-haired gentleman; Francesca, his wife, a
much younger, rather affected sort of woman,
who had never before sat on a horse and lost
no time in telling the others that she was
"absolutely terrified".

"Why did you come then?" Jake asked, slight irritation in his voice. "We like people to come along for the fun of it."

"My husband insisted," Francesca explained, with a a loving glance at Victor that suggested their marriage was not of long standing. "He is such a marvellous horseman. Simply unbeatable in the saddle, aren't you darling?"

Victor modestly conceded that he was. However, such information can be dangerous to give in a riding stable, as the staff may be tempted, as Jake and Andy were, to give you their most difficult mount. Victor was fitted out with a young Connemara cross that had only just been broken and could do with a free training session by an expert hand. Francesca, meanwhile, was mounted on a lazy old nag who would not take a step in any direction unless he had a herd to follow.

Then there were the two youngish girls, Sophie and Marie, both blonde and pretty, Sophie slightly more so than Marie, and both rather on the hefty side, Marie slightly more so than Sophie.

"This one had better take Topper," Andy said with a gesture towards Marie. Topper was a sturdy cob with massive bone, acquired for the benefit of overweight trekkers.

Jake gave him a glare of warning. He had made the same mistake the previous week, telling a very fat American girl that Topper was the only steed strong enough to carry her weight. The girl, offended, had insisted that she was no heavier than anyone else and would only come along if she was given one of the lighter, more elegant mounts. As a result, her poor horse, after only a mile or so, had lain down on the verge panting and refused to go any further. The whole ride had been ruined.

But these girls did not seem to suffer from any such hang-ups, they were jolly and laughing, and once the trek was on the move, the brothers lost no time in chatting them up with a view to taking them out for a drink that evening. A good variety of female company was the perk that had eventually tipped the scales in favour of the project for Jake, and foreign girl trekkers were usually rather taken with the dashing Connemara horsemen in their smart Western gear.

The last of the trekkers was a lanky young man called Philip with expensive riding clothes and a sour face. Like Victor, he had made no secret of his superior riding ability: he had asked for a fiery horse, a bit of a challenge, "if such a thing exists in a Connemara trekking stable".

Andy was annoyed by his condescending tone. "Give him Rosie," he said under his breath to his brother. "She'll sort him out."

Rosie was a highly-strung mare that Jake had bought on impulse in an auction, seduced by her classy looks. She had soon proved to be less than suitable for trekking, having a surplus of hot blood and a wilful character to go with it. Philip, however, managed her all right, though he did not seem to be enjoying himself very much. But then, Jake thought, he was the type who never really enjoyed anything. Even the few smiles that the girls drew from him came out more like grimaces, as if they hurt.

The girls were great, though. They loved every minute, exclaimed in delight over each new aspect of the sea, the ever-changing seams of turquoise and sapphire cut in a million facets by the glitter of the sun. They wanted to know everything about the countryside they were passing through, and the brothers took pains to make the answers to their questions witty and entertaining, just for the pleasure of hearing the bubbling laughter of their response. "What are the donkeys used for?" they asked. "To carry folks to Mass on Palm Sunday."—

"Why are the fields so small?"—"To save time at hay-making."

Victor and Francesca only had eyes for each other. He was giving her a riding lesson as they went along, while at the same time trying to get his barely-broken mount to go forward in something like a balanced movement: the poor thing was wobbling, not sure on which leg to put the weight of the rider which had suddenly been placed on its back. But it was more important for Victor that Francesca's first ever ride was a success, that it gave her an appetite for more. He told her gently to try and sit up and relax. She was crouching stiffly over the pony's neck, holding on to both the reins and the saddle with an anguished expression, more like a person clinging to the edge of a precipice than someone out to have a good time. The reins were so tight, the animal might as well have been wearing a strait-jacket.

"Lengthen your reins a little," Victor told her, dropping his own to show that, if anything, this made the horse more steady and relaxed. "You need a little leeway for when you want to turn," he explained. "Now make him go to the right. Give your right rein a little tug."

"I can't!" Francesca protested. "I'll fall off!"

"Come now, darling," Victor said indulgently.

"Pulling at the rein won't make you fall off."

"But I daren't take my hands off the saddle!"

It was fortunate that Victor was not placed so that he could see the scornful look on Philip's face, for if he had, he would probably have punched his nose. Philip, in fact, was becoming more miserable by the minute. He, too, had had his eye on the luscious girls and was vexed to see all their attention wasted on the two country boys in their ridiculous cowboy outfits. No one said a word to him, he felt lonely and left out. When he finally decided to give the others a reminder that he, too, existed, he did this in the only way he could think of: by voicing a complaint.

He rudely forced his way in between Andy and Sophie, interrupting what looked like a very private conversation. "How much longer are we going to stay on the road?" he asked disdainfully. "I didn't go on this trek just to amble along like a ninny, I expected some decent riding cross-country."

"Wait till we get to the beach," Andy replied. "You'll have all the excitement you want there."

"But why do we stick to the road? I'd like to have a gallop across there," Philip said, pointing to a flat green space just ahead of them.

"You try that," Andy said and then immediately had to restrain the trekker from doing so. "You try that," he resumed, "and you'll never be seen or heard of again. For that is a bog, with a deep hole in the middle, and it would pull you down, horse and all, and it would be the end of you both."

Philip looked dubiously at the inviting green patch. "It doesn't look boggy to me."

"Well you get off my horse then and cross it," Andy said. "I wouldn't mind seeing the last of you, but I'm damned if I'd let my best horse and saddle go down with you!"

Sophie tittered and Andy winked at her. Philip showed his displeasure by doing a malicious imitation of Andy's rather graceless style in the saddle. But no one laughed because no one was looking.

They were just coming round the big bend in the road by Dohulla when Andy spotted a bay pony coming towards them at a fast gallop. He thought no more of it: stray mares often turned up on the road, sometimes they joined the trek for a mile or two, before going back home again. So the ride continued unperturbed, until Andy suddenly reined in his mount.

"Blow me down!" he cried in an aptly chosen expression. "If it isn't the *cuaifeach*!"

Jake, whose gaze had been held by the sight of Marie's ample backside rolling in the saddle, looked up and found to his dismay that his brother was right. However, a jocular approach was as good a weapon as any for dealing with impending disaster.

"Sit tight everyone!" he called. "Hold on to yer dentures!"

The girls trilled with laughter. Victor did not. He was actually wearing dentures and did not like to have his young wife reminded of the fact.

Cuaifeach pulled himself up short only inches from Marie's mount, which happened to be in front. He took one look at the sturdy cob, quite a bit larger than himself, and seeing that it wasn't a mare but a rival male, got straight up on his hind legs and challenged him to a fight. The cob, being of a placid temperament, made a courteous sparring response, only to discover that rearing up is easier said than done when you carry a dead weight of some fourteen stone on your back. In the event all he managed was some ineffectual shadow boxing. Marie shrieked and laughed. "Sophie!" she called to her friend who was cheering and clapping her hands, "get your camera out! I must have a picture of this!"

"Victor, I'm scared," said Francesca.

To comfort her, Victor put out his hand and placed it over her two, which were gripping the saddle with knuckles that were as white as her face.

"It's all right," he said reassuringly. "They are only playing."

Rosie, Philip's highly-strung mount, the only mare amongst them, was getting great excitement out of the performance. She was quivering all over, and her hooves were moving up and down, as if she were treading water. Philip wisely turned her round, away from the action, but Cuaifeach's attention had already been attracted. In a flash he forgot all about establishing male superiority and, with a delighted shriek, pounced on the mare from behind.

Now Rosie, like all horses, was anatomically unable to see behind her. Likewise, her skills at deduction were very limited. She therefore had no way of knowing that it wasn't a Bengal tiger that had suddenly descended on her rear end. And rather than wait and find out, Rosie played safe and scarpered—all in accordance with her impetuous nature.

Cuaifeach joyfully took up the pursuit. A good race was just what he wanted—much more rewarding than the silly games Molly had insisted on playing. After him came Victor on his barely-broken horse; he had been caught unawares with both hands off the reins, stroking the cheek of his fearful spouse. Now Francesca screamed in terror as she saw him carted away.

Being a good horseman, Victor quickly got a hold of the reins. He knew that his best bet was to sit tight until the horse flagged a little, then gently but firmly bring him back to hand. But hearing his wife's loud cries of distress, he suddenly lost his head and started to saw the bit in the horse's mouth, that is, pull very hard, first at one rein, then at the other, deliberately causing the animal such intense pain that it is forced to respond. It is a desperate measure, to be applied only when all else fails, and Victor would not normally have applied it to such a green horse, whose mouth was still unmade. And the result was not the intended: the animal, feeling the bit cut into the left corner of his mouth, shied away from it in a sharp sideways movement. Few riders could have sat that out. Victor tumbled headlong to the ground, right in front of a bright yellow gorse bush.

All this was witnessed by the remaining

members of the ride. Francesca, in floods of tears, dismounted clumsily and ran to her husband's aid. With her mount in tow, the others followed on horseback.

"He'll be all right," Jake called after her, annoyed by this excessive display of emotion.

But Victor was not all right. He did not get up, he did not even stir. When they reached him, they could hear him groaning. That was one thing, Jake thought; at least he was conscious.

"I need an ambulance," the man moaned weakly.

His wife was inconsolable. She flung herself down on her knees and embraced him until he cried out in agony. She looked up at Jake, her eyes black and reproachful.

"It's our honeymoon," she pronounced slowly, her eyes brimming with tears. "Do you understand? It's our honeymoon."

"I'd reckoned as much," said Andy.

"Will you stay with him while we go for help?" Jake asked.

This, for some reason, made her very angry. "Of course I'll stay! What did you think? That I'd leave him here to die?"

Jake and Andy hurriedly galloped off to a nearby house. They knew the man who lived there, Noel Keaney, he was a good sort. As soon as they explained their predicament, he offered to take the injured man to hospital in Galway in his van.

"We need a stretcher of sorts," said Jake.

Together they looked through Noel's shed. There was an old door that might have done if it hadn't been for all the rusty nails sticking out of it—there was no time to remove them. "What about taking off your own front door?" Andy suggested. "We can put it back for you again afterwards." But Noel had a better idea. He pulled out two eight-foot lengths of two-by-one-inch timber and then rooted around for two empty barley sacks. These he proceeded to thread over the timbers, making a light, yet strong makeshift stretcher.

"Brilliant," said Jake.

They found Victor lying as before, his anxious wife tenderly cradling his head. But when they put down the stretcher next to him, he suddenly came to life.

"What's that?" he demanded, sitting up, pushing Francesca aside.

"It's your stretcher," Andy told him.

"I'd rather wait for the ambulance."

"There are no ambulances in these parts," Jake explained. "It would take them ages to come all the way out here. You could die while you waited for it."

By "you" he meant anyone, not Victor in particular, but Francesca turned away, shaken by a renewed burst of sobs.

Victor, with a resigned look on his face, let himself be lifted on to the barley sacks, and Jake and Andy grabbed hold of the protruding timbers to lift him. A contrary groan rose from the sacks under the strain of Victor's body—they sounded as if they were just about to tear.

"Stop!" Victor commanded. "I'd rather walk than have my skull split open on these stones."

"Well if you can manage as far as the van..." Andy started.

"Noel will take you in to Galway," Jake filled in.

Victor was back on his feet.

"He can take me back to my hotel. But first I want my money back. I'm in a good mind to sue you for damages. God knows what serious injuries I've suffered, and as for my wife's distress..."

Before he got any further, Jake pulled out a wad of notes from his pocket and grudgingly handed over one hundred pounds. Victor then walked stiffly to the van, followed by his despondent wife. Noel watched him, his eyes

round with awe, and then said to the brothers:
"I never thought I'd see the like of Lazarus in
Connemara."

Philip, meanwhile, could no longer complain
about "ambling along like a ninny". Rosie was
going at breakneck speed, though along the
road, not cross-country, spurred on by the
sound of Cuaifeach behind her and, further
back, Victor's horse. Each time she tired and
slowed down and Philip thought he might be
able to stop her, her pursuers came closer,
frightening her into a new spurt.

Anyone who has ever been on a runaway
horse can testify that it is not a pleasurable
experience. No matter how good a rider you
are, once you are out of control you might as
well be sitting astride an express train gone
off its rails. A bolting horse is a real danger,
both to itself and others. It is, in fact,
temporarily insane. Any training or condition-
ing impressed on its walnut-sized brain has
been washed away by a torrent of adrenalin in
its bloodstream, obliterating all self-preserving
instincts bar one: to run, run for its life, as its
early ancestors are said to have run, away from
predators across the vast steppes of Inner Asia.

Philip was aware of all this, and he was
terrified. All he could do was cling helplessly

to the saddle, while the bright Connemara landscape swished past his ears: fields and lakes, houses and turf stacks, and flat green patches just like the one Andy had said was a bog with a hole in it deep enough to swallow both him and the horse. It only needed one slight change of direction...

"Help!" Philip shouted into the crisp salty air. "Somebody help me!"

Cars met him, cars overtook him, some of them foreign, some even bearing the number plates of his own country. "Help me!" he yelled at their open windows, "I need heeelp!" But the tourists just shook their heads in amazement at what they took to be a mad Irishman riding his horse in a very unseemly manner. In the end two local men responded to his plight and parked their cars across the road with the doors open to block the horse's path. That was the worst they could have done: it would drive the mare off the road, into the nearest bog.

"No!" Philip roared as he approached. "Nooo!"

Rosie solved the problem by taking a huge leap over one of the doors. The driver, who was still in the car, shakily put his hand out to close it, only to jump back in fright when Cuaifeach and Victor's horse swiftly followed suit.

How he did it, Philip did not know, but he managed to stay in the saddle, even when the mare suddenly lurched to the right, on to a small boreen. God in Heaven! Philip thought, wherever is she taking me now? But then, to his immense relief, he recognised the gaudy sign advertising O'Briens' Trekking Centre. Rosie galloped on, into the yard, where the wall of the big shed finally brought her to a grinding halt.

Philip dismounted. His chest was heaving just like the mare's flanks, and he found that his legs were no good for standing on. He dropped onto his knees and remained thus for some time, his head swimming, clutched by his hands.

Cuaifeach, who had followed Rosie into the yard, was looking around him in astonishment, as if he wondered what on earth had brought him back to this place. Perhaps he feared that he was in for another breaking session? He was too tired, anyhow, to take any interest in the mare; in fact, all three runaways were still dead beat by the time the O'Brien brothers and the girl trekkers returned. So was Philip, by the look of it: he was flat out on a bale of straw.

"Sorry about this folks," Andy said airily to

his three remaining customers. "Hope it didn't spoil your day."

Jake said nothing. He was put out about the hundred pounds he had had to refund to Victor, and also by the fact that the girls had declined their invitation for the evening, explaining that they were on holiday with their boyfriends, who had spent the day playing golf at Bally-conneely.

"You can all come back for a free ride tomorrow," Andy offered, to forestall any further claims for refunds. But the girls said no, they had to catch a flight at Shannon.

Philip had drawn himself up in a standing position, though his knees were still wobbly. "I want my money back," he said in a low resentful voice. "I have never in my life seen such a useless, unprofessional, cowboy set-up."

Jake gave him his fifty pounds, deeply hurt, not so much by the criticism as by the contemptuous way in which he had spat out the word "cowboy".

"Are you all right?" the girls asked their fellow-trekker.

"Oh sure," he replied bitterly. "I've had 'the experience of a lifetime'. Just like the leaflet promised."

When the O'Briens were alone again, Jake

turned wearily to his brother. "I'm beginning to wonder whether this isn't more trouble than it's worth."

"Oh come on!" Andy cried in alarm. "It's all that dratted stallion's fault. As if he hadn't given us enough hassle!"

"What do we do with him now?" Jake asked. "Shoot him?"

"If only we could," Andy sighed. "Ridding the world of him would sure earn us a place in heaven."

At that moment a rusty old banger and trailer drove up, and Christy came shooting out.

"Have you seen...?" he began but stopped himself as he discovered Cuaifeach standing in the yard, looking out over the gate. "God be with ye!" he cried, grabbing first Andy's, then Jake's hand and pumping them vigorously up and down, up and down, as if he couldn't stop. "I should have known I could rely on ye lads," he went on. "I been so worried...so worried he'd get up to some mischief before I found him. Thanks a million!"

And he rushed off to collect the horse.

Jake and Andy looked at each other in despair.

6

wo girls were racing each other on bicycles up the long slope at Gorteen. They were Doreen and her friend Sheila—a girl of slight build and delicate features, though hardy enough, as the saying goes in Connemara to describe a tough healthy child. You'd want to be hardy to grow up in such a wild place, where the simplest thing, like going to school in the morning, will sometimes turn out to be a fierce battle against the elements.

Every day Sheila travelled on her bicycle the five miles from her home in Murvey to the school in Roundstone and back. This morning it had rained heavily and she had arrived at school dripping wet. Not that she minded. Sheila loved cycling, it was her main, if not her only interest. Her dream was to become

Ireland's first girl cycling champion, and in her new green-and-purple trainer suit and her short curly hair, she felt she was beginning to look the part.

Doreen, too, had got very wet that morning, coming from Inishnee on the bike she had borrowed from her brother Tom. She didn't share her friend's enthusiasm; to her the bicycle was merely a means of transport that enabled her to go and see Cuaifeach every day after school. The exercise was getting her very fit, though not as fit as Sheila, who, as usual, was the first to reach the top of the hill. There she slowed down, waiting for Doreen to catch up, and then the girls rode easily together while getting their breath back. It was quite safe for them to cycle side by side on the narrow road: in the stillness that surrounded them, any approaching car could be heard a long way off, long enough for them to get back into single file. The rain had finally stopped and though the haze was still thick over the mountains, the sun shone dimly over the rocky headland beyond Dog's Bay. The sea was a pale blue-green, diluted, as it were, by so much water, and the white sand on the beaches glinted with a newly washed look. The air, still humid, carried a sweet scent of fresh sea grass and wild honeysuckle.

"How much longer will your pony be stopping at Ballyconneely?" Sheila asked and saw her friend's face light up as it always did whenever anyone mentioned Cuaifeach. Fancy being so crazy about a horse, Sheila thought.

"We're bringing him back Saturday," Doreen replied happily. She was delighted that the three weeks were coming to an end. Christy, explaining that "Molly was taking her time", wanted to keep the stallion for another week, but this Doreen had refused. Having heard about his recent break-out, she couldn't wait to have him safely back home again.

"Oh." Sheila was disappointed. Though the girls did not have many interests in common, she liked Doreen's company for cycling, and now that school was about to break up, she had hoped that the other girl would still have call to be coming her way. Otherwise they did not see much of each other in the holidays; like many children in rural areas, they spent most of their spare time at home with their families. Sheila had five younger brothers and sisters whom she was frequently expected to help look after. A waste of time, in her view, since they were all too young to do any serious cycling.

"The vet is coming on Monday," Doreen

added. "We're having him gelded at long last."

Sheila pondered on this for a moment. "Why do you want to do that to him?" she asked.

Doreen's face took on the stubborn look that sometimes came over her. "Because he is my pony," she said, "and I want him to be mine alone. As long as he is a stallion, there will always be other people after him."

"But he may not want to be gelded," Sheila ventured.

"Of course he does!" Doreen retorted. "It's the only way he and I can have some fun together. Like...like going riding, and doing things with the pony club, and competing at shows..."

"Them are all things you like to do," said Sheila. "How do you know that Cuaifeach will enjoy them? He may hate them, for all you know."

"Oh you don't understand!" Doreen burst out angrily. "You don't know the first thing about ponies! You're just saying that because you don't like riding yourself."

"Well that's just it," said Sheila. "Everyone likes different things. All I can say is, if I were your pony, I'd much rather be a stallion than go to the pony club."

"If you were my pony," Doreen argued, "you'd

be off on that bike of yours!" She suddenly laughed out loud. "Couldn't I see you, with your hooves on the handle-bars, and your tail sticking out behind the saddle!"

At that the other girl laughed too, but Doreen was already serious again. Sheila's words had disturbed her more than she wanted to admit. They reminded her of something the vet had said, when she and her father called in to make the appointment. "Are you quite sure this is what you want to do?" he had asked Doreen. "He's a fine horse, and once the operation is done, you know there is no going back."

Something in his voice had indicated that he had his own views on the matter. But Doreen told him that she had her mind made up.

They were getting close to the turning for Sheila's home, and the girl was debating whether to go straight home or continue with Doreen to Ballyconneely.

"Do you think that woman will be there today?" she asked her friend.

"Who?" Doreen asked, startled out of her brooding.

"The woman what paints," Sheila said impatiently.

"Oh, her," said Doreen, remembering that her friend was dying to meet this extraordinary person. "She wouldn't be there today. She can't paint in the rain."

"Well I be going home, so," said Sheila, and they said goodbye. Just as well, Doreen thought. There was little point in bringing Sheila to see Cuaifeach, she had no interest in him at all and would look on, perplexed, when Doreen petted and talked to him. To her that was probably as strange as the idea of herself petting and talking to her bike. Then, before long, she would get bored and insist that they go on cycling instead. Yes, it was just as well that there would be none of that today. Doreen longed to be with her pony, be alone with him, close to him, so that he could reassure her that she was doing the right thing.

The sun was getting brighter. It was pouring its gold onto the ruffled waters of Ballyconneely Bay and she could feel it burning her cheeks. To the west the sky was a clear blue, promising a fine evening. Perhaps Julia the artist would be there after all.

It was on an afternoon just like this about a week before that Doreen had arrived at the field where Cuaifeach and Molly were, to discover a woman seated on a shooting-stick by the gate. In front of her was an easel and she had a palette in one hand and a brush in the other. Coming closer, Doreen was amazed to see a stunning likeness to her stallion staring out at her from the canvas on the easel.

"You're painting Cuaifeach!" she exclaimed.

The woman turned round. "Is that his name?"

"He's my pony," Doreen told her proudly.

"Is he indeed? Then I must congratulate you. He is really beautiful."

That broke the ice as far as Doreen was concerned. Any admirer of Cuaifeach was immediately classified as a friend.

The stallion, hearing his owner's voice, had come trotting up to the gate to greet her. Mud from the wet field splattered from under his hooves, two large splodges landed on the canvas.

"Oh look!" Doreen cried, "he has ruined your picture!"

The woman smiled. "It will dry," she said, "and then I can brush it off. I had done enough for one day, anyhow."

She wiped her brush on a cloth and started to put the paints away in a case.

"I wish I could paint like that," said Doreen, stealing a last glance at the picture before climbing the gate to join her pony.

"Oh but you've got the real thing," said the woman. "That's much better."

She stayed and chatted while Doreen made much of Cuaifeach, smiled sympathetically at his show of affection. He was a different pony now since he was let out, friendly and easy-going, and pleased to see Doreen whenever she came. Before long, he realised that he was the main object of their conversation and, having had his fill of fondling, gave them a little performance, galloping around the field, bucking and gambolling, and then looking back to see if they were watching. As he approached Molly, he got up on his hind legs and took several steps like that towards her. The old mare ignored him to the extent of not even lifting her head up from grazing.

"He's got a hard match on his hands there," said the woman.

"Do you know a lot about horses?" Doreen asked.

"Well..." said the woman with the kind of modesty that only knowledgeable people display. "I've lived with them for many years."

After that they had met several times. The woman told Doreen that she normally lived in England but had taken a cottage at Lower

Errislannan for the summer and was hoping to get on with her painting. She asked the girl to call her Julia, which Doreen found awkward at first, but then it occurred to her that the woman could hardly be much older than her eldest sister. She was, in fact, not unlike Brid: tall and slim, with her brown hair pulled back in a ponytail. She was more reserved, though, and gentler, somehow, than Brid, whose brisk, cheerful manner could sometimes border on the bullying. "I wouldn't like to be one of her patients," their father used to say jokingly. Brid worked as a geriatric nurse in Manchester.

Cuaifeach liked Julia too—that was obvious from the way he arranged himself in all manners of striking poses whenever she put her easel up. The only problem, the artist complained, was that he never stayed still long enough for her to sketch him.

Doreen told her Uncle Christy about her new friend, but he, it turned out, was already well-informed.

"She's a queer one," he said disapprovingly. "What is a fine figure of a woman like her doing cooped up in a cottage in Errislannan? She should have a husband to look after, and a houseful of kids!"

"She paints," Doreen explained in a loyal

attempt to defend her.

"Paints, my foot!" Christy snorted. "That's not what women are supposed to be doing."

Doreen had to admit that she, too, found it rather odd that a nice, attractive woman like Julia should not have managed to find a husband for herself. Though she had sisters who had gone their own way, she herself was stuck, like her grand-uncle, in the old-fashioned system to which her mother, and all her friends' mothers, strictly subscribed. With the lack of employment opportunities, marriage was one of the few options open to Connemara women apart from emigration, and their large families kept them busy at home for most of their working life. Likewise, the established division of labour between husband and wife was never questioned: you couldn't expect an often pregnant woman to be out digging ditches or dipping sheep while the man stayed at home making bread and minding the little ones.

But then one day, the mystery surrounding Julia's marital status was clarified. She told Doreen she had been to the Galway races and had met some of her old friends there. Did she go racing a lot in England? Doreen asked. Julia said she used to go with her husband. So she had one after all! And not only did she have one—she also revealed that he had been a jockey.

"Is that so?" Doreen exclaimed. "Oh I've always wanted to meet a real jockey! Will he be coming here?"

A shadow fell over Julia's face. "He's not around," she said, and then she added lightly, almost casually, as if she wanted to take the edge off the words: "He died last year."

"Oh..." Doreen's voice was full of commiseration. "How awful for you."

She did not shy away from death with horror or embarrassment, coming as she did from a place where it was accepted as an inevitable part of life and shared by everyone, from the youngest to the oldest. Wakes, removals, funerals were attended by people in their hundreds: Doreen had been to more of them than she could remember. And like all members of her community, she knew the rules surrounding such occasions, knew how to express sympathy, how to help the bereaved by talking to them about the person they had lost.

"Was it an accident?" she asked Julia. "Did he have a bad fall?"

"No..." Julia replied, taken aback but also warmed by the girl's frank interest. "It would perhaps have made more sense that way...I mean, I was always prepared for that. But he just got ill and died. It was over in a few weeks."

Then she talked more about him, prompted by Doreen's breathless attention. He had died at the age of thirty-four, Eric O'Reilly, one of Britain's top jockeys, known for his magical touch with horses. He had never forced them, hardly ever used his whip, and yet he managed to get the very best performance out of every mount he rode. He was of Irish descent, and for many years he had been talking to his wife about the holiday they would have one day in Connemara, the most beautiful part of his native country, where his childhood summers had been spent tearing around bareback on wild Connemara ponies. But the journey had never been made and now she had come on her own to finally see the place they used to dream about.

"And is it like you expected it?" Doreen asked.

"Oh yes." Julia smiled. "Everything is just the way he described it."

Her sadness was gone, it was as if a light was shining within her. And Doreen had a feeling that, from this day, their friendship would deepen.

She stopped off at Keogh's shop to pick up some groceries for Uncle Christy, who was confined to bed with a bad bout of summer flu. When she entered the cottage, she found him lying, as he had been for the last couple of days, in the settle bed over in the corner, shivering under layers of blankets. He wore a blue woollen hat, and his eyes and his nose were red.

"How are you today?" Doreen asked, putting down her shopping bag.

"Not so good, not so good," Christy moaned.

He took his health very seriously.

The fire had gone out, and the cottage was dank and cold, as old stone buildings tend to be after a wet day, even in summer. Doreen raked out the ashes and filled the turf-bin before lighting a new fire and putting the kettle on.

"Bless you, my girleen," came feebly from over by the bed, followed by an extended fit of coughing.

"Do you want me to get the doctor?" Doreen wondered.

"Doctor?" Christy, at the mere mention of the word, suddenly perked up. "I never seen a doctor in my life, and if I did, it would surely kill me."

"But the doctor would get you well," Doreen protested.

"Doctors and priests, they're all the same," Christy muttered. "They come when all hope is out...getting them sooner is bad luck."

"Why is it bad luck?"

"Oh you know," Christy said impatiently. "You must never act like you're in a hurry to depart from this life. You may be taken up on it. I seen it happen, time and again."

Rather than argue the point, Doreen changed tack. "Do you know if Julia is here today?"

"And how would I know, lying here on me own all day?" said Christy. "It's not as if she'd be in here tucking up me blankets. God save me if she did," he mused, "because"—his voice dropped to a conspiratorial whisper—"they say she's come to Connemara to find herself a new husband."

"What rubbish," was Doreen's reaction. "She tells me she has an awful bother with the local bachelors who want to take her out for drinks in the evenings. She wouldn't dream of accepting but at the same time she doesn't want to give offence."

"Sure now," said Christy, in a tone that

betrayed a wealth of bitter experience, "she's one of them like to do their own picking. I know the kind well."

"I think you can feel quite safe, Uncle Christy," said Doreen. "You're much too old for her."

"I'm lucky so," her grand-uncle concluded.

Leaving him with four large ham sandwiches, which he insisted he could not possibly touch but she knew he would soon eat, Doreen hurried out and down the track, between thick fuchsia hedges, towards the field gate. She could see Julia's white car parked down there and Julia herself on her way up to the gate.

She suddenly stopped short. It had come to her in a flash that something was not right. And when Julia turned towards her, the expression on her face confirmed Doreen's worst misgivings. She wanted to call out, ask her what was the matter, but not a word would pass over her lips.

"Look at Cuaifeach," Julia said in a low voice. "There's something wrong with him."

The stallion was standing at the far end of the field. His head was hanging so low it almost touched the ground, the ears were slack and his eyes stared dull and sunken into space. His stomach was tucked up hard underneath him, and on his neck was a large dark patch of sweat.

"Oh Julia," Doreen said thickly, the words sticking in her throat, "he looks awful sick."

"Yes," Julia agreed. "He's not well at all."

They climbed over the gate and rushed up to him, passing Molly who grazed contentedly, acknowledging their presence only by pointing her ears. There was no such reaction from Cuaifeach. He stood as if enclosed in his own suffering, alone in a world where nothing else mattered.

Doreen called his name, held out her hand to touch him, but he still did not respond. Then Julia discovered that the grass under his head was stained red. She went round in front of him and bent down to examine his mouth. There was blood on his muzzle, and the upper lip was so swollen the mouth did not close properly. Very gently Julia parted his lips, expecting resistance, but there was none. What she saw made her cry out in horror. Doreen, who had her arms around his neck, looked up.

"What is it?"

"Don't look, Doreen," Julia said. "You wouldn't want to."

"I have to see," the girl cried, coming round to kneel in front of him while Julia still held his mouth open. Oh it was worse, much worse than anything she could have imagined! His upper jaw was a gory mass of torn flesh and broken bone and fragments of his front teeth— his healthy young teeth splintered like crushed nuts—were embedded in the gums, some so deep that only a small chip showed, surrounded by tender blue inflammation.

"How could this have happened?" Doreen asked in a small voice. It was her only rational thought: how could it have happened?

"It's that wicked old mare," Julia said with a resentful glare at Molly, who looked back, apparently rather pleased with herself. "Doreen, she's kicked his teeth in."

Doreen started to cry.

"It could have been worse," Julia consoled her. "It won't kill him, the vet will be able to put him right."

"But he's in such agony," Doreen wept. "And it's all my fault, for letting him come here. Oh my poor, poor Cuaifeach!"

Julia said she would drive over to Keogh's to call the vet. The girl stayed with her pony, devastated by his agony and by her own inability to relieve it. She stood close to him, stroking his neck, away from where it hurt, but his lack of response left her with a feeling that he would never ever forgive her.

Then, almost imperceptibly, the stallion leant sideways onto her. She staggered at first under his weight, but then set all of her strength against it. She could feel her heart pounding against the bulk of his shoulder and then it missed a beat as his message to her came through: sick though he was, he was still leaning on her, relying on her to help him. Whoever was to blame for what had happened, he had not lost his trust in her.

"Oh Cuaifeach," she whispered. "I promise you'll be all right again. Your pain will soon be over."

This time his ears flickered.

The sun was sinking in the sky but it still shone on the two of them, kept them warm. And though the pony's suffering was still as bad, it seemed to the girl that he was just a little bit less miserable.

In the meantime, Julia had managed to get through to the vet on his mobile telephone. He was appalled when he heard what had happened. Poor chap, he kept saying, poor chap, in an outraged voice, as if it was a close friend of his that had been assaulted. Unfortunately he was far from them—way down South Connemara—but he gave Julia his instructions, and she acted promptly upon them.

The keys were in the door of Christy's cottage, and when there was no answer to her knock, Julia pushed the door open and entered. The old man was asleep but at the sound of her footsteps on the concrete floor, he woke up and peered at her with feverish, red-rimmed eyes.

"I must be sicker than I thought," he mumbled, "to be seeing visions..."

"I'm sorry to bother you," Julia began briskly but stopped herself when she discovered a look of sheer terror on the old man's face.

"I'm no good to you," he averred in a weak, quivering voice. "No good to you at all."

"I've only come to ask you a favour," Julia declared in what she hoped was a calm, reassuring manner. "You know who I am, don't you?"

"I'm an old man," he protested. "And I'm not well, either." He coughed loudly for the point to strike home.

Julia had no more time for this nonsense. "Cuaifeach has been injured," she told him firmly. "He has been kicked by that mare of yours."

That made Christy sit up. "Badly?" he asked.

"Yes, it is quite bad. He has to have an emergency operation."

"God forgive her!" Christy croaked. "But then, he should have known better."

"I need to borrow your trailer," Julia went on. "To take him to the vet."

"Leave that to me!" Christy said, jumping out of bed. He was fully dressed, shoes and all, under the blankets. But once he got to his feet, he became so dizzy that he had to hold on to the doorpost to steady himself.

Julia assured him that she could manage with Doreen. Her car had a tow-bar, and she was used to transporting horses. In the end Christy was quite relieved to be allowed back to his bed, where he tried to dispel his mounting sense of guilt by repeating to himself: "He should have known better. Females are bad enough when they are after something... when they want nothing from you, they are altogether deadly. Oh, he should have known better!"

Cuaifeach let himself be led by Doreen into the trailer without protests. Then they drove very gently on the bumpy roads the long way to the vet's surgery in Moycullen, where he had agreed to meet them.

"I suppose there is one good thing to come

out of this," Julia said reflectively.

"What?" Doreen wondered.

"He won't be able now to have his operation on Monday."

Some Victory

7

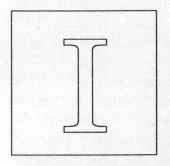t was the second Sunday in July, the day of the Ballyconneely Show, and a good crowd had gathered in the showground, a nice flat field behind the church, with well over a hundred ponies. "Grand day," people were saying to each other, "a grand day for a show." The weather picture was one of large woolly clouds whipped by a brisk north-westerly across a deep blue sky—not great, though common enough in Connemara in summer. But it was ideal for a show: not too warm and sunny to lure people away to the beaches, not too wet and windy to keep them indoors.

The show had started almost on time and now the third class, for yearling fillies, was in full swing. The first two classes, for yearling and two-year-old colts, had been the usual disappointment: few breeders were prepared to hold on to their colts with all the difficulties it entailed, and of the ones entered, not all had turned up. A couple had not made it in time; their owners had assumed that the show, like most Connemara fixtures, would get off to a late start.

The filly class, by contrast, was well attended: no less than fourteen young mares were being paraded in the ring. Friends, rivals and a number of slightly perplexed tourists watched from ringside, as the proud owners walked their ponies round, round, under the judges' critical gaze.

Doreen had arrived with her parents but soon teamed up with Julia, who had never been to a Connemara pony show before, Ballyconneely being the first in the season. She had many questions to ask her young but well-informed friend. Why were some of the fillies so much larger and more developed than the others? They were the ones that had been kept in sheds since they were weaned, Doreen explained, they had been kept in and given loads of concentrates to promote their growth. "Like pigs being fattened for Christmas?" Julia asked dubiously. She could see that, in most cases, the goodness of the food had gone to their heads: they were leaping about excitedly, rearing and bucking, one even managed to pull her owner, a big burly man, off his feet. It probably wasn't long ago, Julia reflected, that farmers in this part of the world couldn't afford to feed their ponies at all in winter, but had to see them starve and suffer. No wonder then that they saw nothing wrong in stuffing them with all the food they could eat. But to her, overfeeding a pony whilst denying it exercise was almost as cruel as making it work hard on an empty stomach. Didn't they notice the red glint of madness in the pony's eye, which, once established, might stay with it for ever?

At the other end of the scale were the fillies that, according to Doreen, "had been brought up the old way": left on mountain and commonage to fend for themselves and generally run wild. Paradoxically, these were the tame ones. They walked along in a mannerly way, stepping out freely with hard, athletic bodies, although, it must be admitted, they looked notably immature compared with their more pampered rivals.

So which type would the judges favour? Julia couldn't wait to see. But then, she might have guessed: there had to be some reason why ponies should be kept in such unnatural conditions. Of the six fillies pulled up for prizes, only one was of the small, hardy variety—but she had so much quality, they simply couldn't have passed her over. The biggest and fattest of the lot did not get anywhere. She had to be sent out of the ring due to unruly behaviour, including trying to kick the judge.

People kept coming up to Doreen to enquire about Cuaifeach's health. The news of his misfortune had spread, courtesy of Johnny Tass, to every corner of Connemara. "A terrible thing," they mumbled, "a terrible thing to happen." Doreen told them he was well on the mend, the vet had done a great job, there would be no lasting damage. But he had lost a lot of condition while he was sick and couldn't eat and it would be a while before he picked up again. "Pity," they said, shaking their heads, "pity on such a fine horse." No one referred to him as being wild and obstreperous, now he was just "the poor horseen".

The two-year-old filly class also had a huge entry. The judges, give them their due, asked to see each one trotted up individually rather than send the inferior ones out of the ring straight away. But it was a long, time-consuming process, and most of the tourists got bored and drifted off to buy ice-cream. Finally, the line-up was settled. At the tail end was Tom Samuel with a filly as shaggy and neglected as could be expected. He and his cousin Joe Will had walked the long way from their home in the Bens with a string of four ponies, the best of their herd, though that did not mean much. They had set out at the crack of dawn, amid birdsong and scattered showers, convinced, as always, that chance would be on their side.

Everyone, for once, was delighted to see the winner of this class and agreed that "the prize couldn't have gone to a better man". It was Bernard, who had so sadly lost his lovely grey mare, showing a gorgeous two-year-old the colour of cream toffee.

"She's the daughter of the mare that got killed," Johnny Tass informed the bystanders. "Bernard had her sold as a foal, but he travelled all the way to Mullingar to find the man and managed to buy her back."

"She done well on the rich grass up country," Marty MacDonagh observed expertly. "She's every bit as good as the mother."

Even better, he thought to himself, but he did not say so, out of deference to the dead mare.

In the three-year-old class it was Joe Will's turn to be last.

"Why do those two bother to show their animals at all?" Julia asked. "You'd have thought they'd know better."

"They come along for the crack," Doreen explained. "They don't seem to mind losing."

And sure enough, Joe Will's toothless grin was as broad as ever. The same could not be said of some of the other contestants down the line: Jake O'Brien, who was second last, wore a formidable scowl that was in sharp contrast to his sanguine neighbour.

One smartly-dressed man was walking through the crowd with an uneasy, somewhat lost look on his face, as if he wasn't used to being amongst so many people. The truth was that he was well used to crowds, but only as the focus of their attention. Here nobody even looked at him, no fingers were pointed, no kids asked for his autograph. They all seemed more interested in the ponies, he noted with surprise. It did not occur to him that it was merely for the sake of the ponies that they had all gathered there.

He was Roc O'Neill, swimming star of the Seventies, Olympic Gold Medallist and for many years Ireland's pride on the international swimming circuit. His real name was Declan, but he had been known as Roc, Irish for ray, ever since a sports journalist early on in his career had likened his aggressive onslaught in the water to the behaviour of a hooked ray. His success had not been restricted to swimming: he had also made himself a fortune selling swimming-pools to all the smart home-owners around Dublin with the slogan: "No home is complete without a *Roc Pool*."

Now middle-aged, he had retired to Connemara, where he had set up a luxurious leisure centre just north of Roundstone. Roc's Harbour on the edge of the Atlantic offered "holidays for health". You could swim in a giant-size Roc pool with water pumped up from the sea and heated to a Mediterranean temperature, you could windsurf and sail, go fishing or play golf or work-out in a splendidly appointed gym. At night you danced away your surplus pounds in the nightclub disco. The project had met with a mixed response from the local community: there had been objections at the planning stage from certain individuals who felt that the complex was too large and intrusive in the unspoilt landscape. But others, and the authorities with them, had decided that such a major capital investment could only benefit the area, especially since Roc had committed himself to recruiting his entire labour force from the West. Now in its first season, Roc's Harbour employed over fifty people and showed every sign of being a success.

Roc had no interest whatsoever in ponies. He had come along to the Ballyconneely Show just to watch his son Dominic win the riding class. Dominic was his only child by his estranged wife and was spending the summer holidays with his father. He was crazy about horses and had even got himself a job for the summer helping out at the O'Briens' Trekking Centre up the road from them. Roc thought it ridiculous that the lad could not find enough to occupy him at the leisure centre—what boy had a playground like that at his feet?—but as long as it kept him happy, Roc let it pass. However, not wanting to lose the boy completely, he had made an agreement with the O'Briens, whereby trekking was added to the list of facilities available to his guests.

He suddenly caught sight of Jake's Stetson bobbing in the crowd and went up to join him, pleased to see someone he knew. Jake was talking to a group of local men, rough and weatherbeaten, wearing cloth caps and woolly hats though it was the middle of the summer.

They nodded casually as Roc was introduced,
almost as if he had been one of them. To Roc
this was an unusual experience. Normally
people treated him either with adulation, or
else with a strange sort of aggression, as if they
resented his celebrity status. These fellows
were tolerant and unimpressed. Roc found it
quite relaxing.

Jake was apparently in the middle of a
heated discussion about the judging of the
show. "I'd like to know what these guys are
looking for," he said in a loud angry voice. "I
mean, how can they give an award to something like that?"

He pointed to Tom Samuel, who was
triumphantly leading around his scruffy colt,
the one that had been turned down at Maam
Cross. The pony had a bright yellow rosette
attached to his filthy rope halter.

"Ah," said one of the men, "that was because
there were only three of them in the class. They
had to give it to him."

They were joined by a dejected-looking man,
Paddy Pat from Cashel, who had failed to
secure a ribbon for his best mare in the three-
year-old class.

"It's always the same people what win," he
sighed. "You'd think the judges look more at

the owners than at the ponies."

"You're sure right," said Jake warmly. "They never looked at my mare at all, just packed me off down the line."

"There was a man one year at a show," Johnny Tass told them, "who wanted to put the judges to the test. He made a bet with a sure prize-winner, and they exchanged ponies before going into the ring. What do you think happened? The man what used to win got first with the middling pony, and the one what made the bet got nowhere at all with the good one."

Marty MacDonagh pursed his lips disapprovingly. "There's nothing wrong with the judging," he said primly. "It takes a long time to develop an eye for a good pony. The judges see things other people are blind to."

"He has to say that," Paddy Pat confided to Roc O'Neill, "because he always wins."

Marty got even more annoyed. "The judges here today are as honest as they come," he said. "They're not afraid of standing by their own opinion. Who else would have dared pull the reigning Clifden Champion down to fourth place?"

This, they all agreed, was a very brave thing to do. The pony's owner had been so incensed that he had thrown back his prize in the judges' faces and told them what he thought of their ability. It was an amusing intermezzo that had livened up the show for all of them.

"You tell me then why I did so badly," Jake said to Marty. "What was wrong with my pony?"

"Not enough condition," Marty replied simply.

"She's covered in muscle, for Chrissake!" Jake protested. "Fat ponies are no good for working."

"Working ponies never win," Marty informed him. "They are too lean."

"But that's what they're there for..." Jake started. He was interrupted by the loudspeaker announcing the start of the first riding class. "We'd better go," he said to Roc, "and see how Dominic and Andy are doing."

Roc was relieved. He felt slightly dizzy by all the pony talk. He had never spent so long in conversation without the word swimming being mentioned once.

The riding classes were held in a different field, one that sloped some forty-five degrees, which made it far from ideal for riding, but as usual the in-hand classes had taken priority. There were two classes, one for children under twelve, one for children over twelve. Dominic was twelve, so he could have entered either— or both, Andy had suggested, but that, Roc protested, would not be correct. So they had settled for the junior class, where his victory would be most certain. This was the one that was just beginning.

There were five contestants altogether, which was deemed to be a good turn-out. Children in Connemara are surrounded by ponies from the moment they are born, but these animals are used mainly for breeding and only rarely broken and ridden. Dominic was on one of the O'Brien ponies, a chestnut mare that looked a darned sight more elegant, Roc noted with satisfaction, than the other pit ponies. Dominic, too, looked great. He was certainly the best turned out of all the kids— and the most expensively, Roc thought grimly to himself, remembering the bill that had just come in from the tack-shop in Galway. But it was not only that. His lanky body, which sometimes struck Roc as being weedy, looked smart and erect in the saddle. It brought to mind an old-fashioned cavalry officer. The other riders, by comparison, looked like sacks of potatoes. And he rode well, even Roc could see that. He had of course had umpteen riding lessons in one of Dublin's top riding stables. Another big bill. Roc could certainly well afford it, and he wasn't mean, just amazed that riding cost so much money, and that the world obviously was full of fools prepared to pay for it. Swimming, after all, could be had at the price of a pair of togs. Still, it was worth a lot to him to see the exultant, confident look on Dominic's face. Roc smiled. If there was one thing he wanted to give his son, it was the sweet taste of winning.

Andy had come up to them. "He sure is a fine sight," he said to Roc, indicating Dominic. "You can be proud of him."

Roc gave his son an appreciative wink and nod as he trotted past them, and saw the lad blush with pleasure. Poor kid, he suddenly thought to himself, it can't be easy to have me as a father to live up to. It's high time he had some success of his own.

One of the pit ponies, with a sack of potatoes on top, was pulled in, and then another, and another. Dominic was the last to be called in. This, Roc concluded, must mean that they left the winner till last. But then they proceeded to hand the first pony a red rosette, and a trophy! This couldn't be right! Dominic couldn't be last, he couldn't be. He rode better, looked better than any of the others...was it a fix?

"What the heck's going on?" he asked Jake and Andy.

The brothers, as flabbergasted as he was, mumbled something deprecatingly about not understanding a thing. Rosie was their best pony, Dominic had done great. They had been convinced he would win.

As soon as the class was over, Roc got hold of the judge, a short, stout woman, who seemed to become even shorter and stouter when confronted by Roc's towering athletic frame.

"Will you explain this!" the swimming star commanded in front of a curious crowd that quickly drew up around them. "Why did my son come last? What did he do wrong that the others didn't?"

The judge only had to take one look at Roc's designer leisure wear to connect him with the well-dressed boy on the chestnut mare.

"He didn't do anything wrong," she replied politely. "I thought he rode very well."

"So why did he lose?" Roc boomed. "You have some explaining to do."

"Well it's not the riding that is awarded," the judge told him, "it's the pony. Your son's mount was too light of bone."

"You mean you prefer that socking big thing

over there?" Roc said, pointing to the winner. "It looks awful to me, and the girl could do with a few riding lessons."

"It is a good exponent of the Connemara breed," the judge said equably. "Plenty of bone, top condition, good paces. As I said, the riding isn't the main thing."

"It is a riding class, for God's sake!" Roc shouted.

"It is a Connemara class," the judge retorted and went back into the ring, where the contenders for the second class were waiting.

Dominic, still astride his pony, stood a little way off, looking pale and frightened. His father strode up to him with Jake and Andy in tow.

"Get off that pony," Roc ordered. "We're going home."

✤✤✤

After watching the riding class, Julia and Doreen went down to the community hall, where trestle tables and benches had been erected and tea was being served with sandwiches and homemade cakes. It was now well into the afternoon and the hall was packed with hungry customers but they managed to find two vacant seats in a corner near the ladies' toilet.

"We should have brought Cuaifeach," Julia said. "I'm sure he would have had a good chance in the stallion class."

Doreen shook her head knowingly. "Not the way he is now. It will be a long time before I have him back in show condition."

Her head drooped as she thought of the long, arduous task of nursing the pony back to health. Getting him to eat well, without fear of pain, had been the main problem. The vet had recommended grass, sweet succulent grass, but the one field they had was fenced in only by a stone wall, and they were still in the height of the season. Even at the time when Cuaifeach was too weak to jump out, mares could have jumped in to pester him. So Doreen had spent the first part of her summer holidays sitting in the field with Cuaifeach on a long rope. When it rained, as it often did, she sat inside the shed, about as bored as Cuaifeach had been there all winter. But he did love the grass that he had been without for so long, and his swift recovery, as well as his obvious relish, made every effort worthwhile.

"He's young still," Julia reflected. "You'll probably do better with him next year."

"He won't be a stallion then," Doreen

reminded her.

Julia said nothing in reply. She thought it would be a crime to geld Cuaifeach but she knew Doreen's reasons and did not want to put any pressure on her.

"If I ever show him, it will be in the riding class," the girl continued, and then she added dejectedly: "Though right now I feel as if I shall never get on his back. Everything is against me."

The vet had told her that the pony could not be castrated until he got over his injuries. But now that he was more or less recovered, the fly season had set in, and with it, an increased risk of infection. It would have to be September, the vet had said. September! Just when Doreen was due to go back to school!

"Now may be as good a time as any to break him," Julia suggested. "He's gone very quiet since the accident."

"I asked Uncle Christy," Doreen told her, "but he says no one will take him on unless he is gelded."

"I might," Julia said gently.

Doreen stared at her for a moment, while she took this in. Then her eyes began to shine. "Do you think you could?"

Julia smiled. "Eric used to say, there's

nothing so easy as breaking a horse. For if it isn't easy, then you can be sure you're doing something wrong."

"If that is so," Doreen mused, "the O'Briens must have got an awful lot wrong."

They laughed. Johnny Tass had had them both in stitches only a couple of days before, giving them a blow-by-blow account of the O'Briens' breaking venture.

"I would use a slightly different approach," Julia assured her. "Best of all would be if you were there to help me."

The girl hesitated briefly. "My parents won't let me ride him until he is fully broke."

"That's okay," said Julia. "I'll be on his back. You'll be more use to me on the ground. They won't object to that, will they?"

"Surely not," Doreen laughed. "I'm on the ground all the time, aren't I?"

As they returned to the showground, they met a man on his way out with a mare. He wore a face like an old boot, and the pony, amazingly, looked equally disenchanted. They were Marty MacDonagh and Veronica, the champion mare, Cuaifeach's mother, who had come out of her class sporting a blue, not a red, rosette.

"Honest judges here today," someone called

after him. "As honest as they come!"

His laughter was echoed by some of the others, but Marty and Veronica were not amused.

In the ring, the class for mares over twenty years of age was in progress. One man was trotting his pony up in front of the judges. He was limping badly.

"Whatever happened to Brendan's leg?" a man at ringside asked another. "He was all right this morning."

"Oh he always puts on a limp when he shows that mare," was the reply. "It's the mare goes down on her near fore, and he believes his own limping will mask it."

"Most judges are fooled," a third man put in. "He's won a championship with her that way."

But today's judges were not taken in. Brendan was relegated to a place well down the line, next to Joe Will who, for the first time this day, was not last—he was beaten to it by a certain Molly, who had failed to impress the judges, even though the opposition was confined to eleven other old grandmothers.

"I know it's not very high-minded of me," Julia whispered, "but I can't say I'm sorry."

Doreen had to laugh, though she realised

what a blow this must be to her uncle. "It's divine justice," she said. "I'm only sorry Cuaifeach isn't here to gloat at her."

The show's main attraction, the stallion class, was the last of the day. This was for reasons of safety, to get mares, foals and youngstock out of the way beforehand. Ranks were closed as the parade entered: six magnificent beasts, stepping high, snorting and snarling, swishing their tails. Perhaps they weren't quite as ferocious as they appeared—but this was how people liked to see them, and their handlers—all men, of course, strong masculine fellows—obliged by treating them with enough aggression to tease out their most impressive behaviour. Chains were rattled, sticks raised: the stallions pawed the ground, bared their teeth and reared up. It was a little like watching lion-tamers at work.

Christy was watching, his heart down in his boots. Why had he humiliated himself by bringing old Molly to the show? This was the class he should have been in, he should have brought Doreen's horse, got him to put on his best—that is, his worst—manners. Christy would have shown them all that he was as good a man as any, even though he wasn't getting any younger.

He overheard some men talking behind him. "Cuaifeach isn't here today," one of them remarked. "Oh that one," another sneered contemptuously, "didn't you hear, he got himself kicked to pieces by a sour old mare." There was a chortle. "Kicked? By a mare? Wasn't he supposed to be the most savage of them all?" "Not any more, he's gone as meek as a lamb, runs away at the sight of a mare. He'll never be any good as a stallion."

Christy turned round. "Cuaifeach," he said indignantly, "is every bit as wild as he used to be. An accident could happen to anyone."

But they did not take any notice.

"Look at Malachy's horse," one man said admiringly. "He is a real handful. I had to give a hand the other day, to help get him shod."

"Who was the blacksmith?" someone wanted to know.

"Seamus O'Toole, of course. No one else would go near him. But even he had problems, you know, the horse wouldn't stand for him, kept pushing him around the stable. In the end Seamus got mad and belted him in the ribs with the rasp. That's when all hell broke loose. The stallion went for him."

"So what happened?" another man asked breathlessly.

The first man chuckled. "I'll tell you one thing: I never saw a man out so fast over a half-door."

Christy once more turned to face them. "If that had been Cuaifeach," he said proudly, "the blacksmith would have gone through the door."

No one was surprised when the class was won by a well-known eighteen-year-old stallion owned by the Connemara Pony Breeders' Society. This horse was expected to go on to win the championship, which was open to winners of all classes— he had won many shows before. But yet again the judges made an unexpected, independent choice. The champion of the show turned out to be the toffee-coloured winner of the two-year-old filly class.

To thunderous applause, which frightened some of the ponies, Bernard received the large silver cup and held it up high over his head for everyone to see, while the judges draped the broad ribbon over the filly's neck. It was an outcome that appealed to the crowd, left them with a pleasant aftertaste, suggesting that there was some justice in this world after all. And as people left the showground in the light of the evening sun, tired, hungry and thirsty after their long day out, they were all in agreement that this year's show in Ballyconneely had been the best ever.

8

f Eric O'Reilly's words
were anything to go by,
Julia and Doreen must
have got everything right from the start, for
the initial process of breaking Cuaifeach could
not have been simpler. Breaking wasn't really
the right word for it, Julia said, it was all a
matter of tuning in with the horse, spending
enough time with him, listening to him,
interpreting his signals, making your own
intentions clear and then just waiting until he
was ready to go along with them.

On the Monday after the Ballyconneely
Show they took him in Christy's trailer from
Inishnee to Julia's garden. It was well-fenced,
and the people who looked after the cottage
did not mind at all. The garden had been left
to grow wild since the owners went to Australia

and if anything it would benefit from his grazing. Cuaifeach settled down at once, delighted to indulge in the lush grass of the lawn and pick at the variety of plants and shrubs.

Julia's first objective was simply to get closer to him, and to achieve this she spent the first couple of days with him in the garden. She set up her easel and got to work on a new picture; sitting down and keeping still was a good idea because it made her seem less of an intrusion to the horse. She never went up to him at all but waited for his approach, and sure enough, he soon became curious and came up to sniff her and her equipment. He even bit into the canvas and left a big uneven mark from his rearranged teeth. When she put out her hand to scratch him, he nibbled at her hair in reply, like one friendly horse to another, and when she went in to have lunch, he came with her to the kitchen door and would probably have followed her in, if she had let him. Instead she handed him a couple of carrots through the open window, and he nibbled them gratefully. Julia was pleased—this was exactly the kind of relationship she had hoped to establish.

She had asked Doreen to leave her alone with Cuaifeach for the first couple of days, but on the Wednesday the girl arrived on her bicycle. Together they drove over to the pony club to borrow a hackamoor bridle, that is, one without a bit, as Julia did not want to worry his mouth so soon after the accident. Doreen was concerned that this might not give her enough control, but Julia told her no control would be necessary. She was only going to ask him to do what he wanted to do himself, when he wanted to do it.

Home again, they put on the hackamoor and saddled him up. It was Julia's saddle; she had brought her own tack from England, in case she came across something suitable to ride. Then they led the stallion out on to the road and over to the little beach some way down from the cottage. It was tiny but each time the tide went out, it exposed a stretch of white sand just large enough and firm enough to serve as training ground. It was wide open, but again, Julia said, she had no intention of giving Cuaifeach a reason to run away. She had already checked that there were no loose mares in this part of Errislannan.

Doreen was leading and Cuaifeach walked along happily. His dog-like devotion to the girl had only deepened during his convalescence, and this was a state that Julia planned to exploit. She herself was walking behind the girl, by the pony's shoulder. Now and then they stopped, and as Doreen made much of him to make him feel good, Julia got in a little closer, touching him, leaning on him, putting some of her weight on his back. Whenever she felt the slightest tension in him, she quickly drew back, though her approach was so careful and sensitive that it did not happen much. She knew what she was waiting for: his total acceptance of her physical presence. Towards the end of the week the moment arrived. "Hold him there," she told Doreen just as they were about to leave the beach. "I can tell he's ready."

She mounted. Cuaifeach did not object, but he turned his head to see what was being done to him. Julia talked to him, holding out her hands and feet for him to see that it was she and not someone less welcome who had suddenly jumped on his back.

"This is about as far as the O'Briens got," Doreen stated. "Not any further."

Taking a gentle hold on the reins, Julia asked Doreen to walk slowly forward. Just as she expected, Cuaifeach followed in the footsteps of his beloved owner though he was a little unsteady on his feet because of the unaccustomed weight on his back. When

Doreen stopped, Julia held him in; when she
started again, Julia urged him forward. That
way her wishes and his own blended into one,
and it never occurred to him to offer any
resistance. Later on, by a transition impercept-
ible to him, his will would be gradually
subordinated to hers: he wouldn't be fully
broken until that process was complete. But
that was a long way down the road. For the
time being, she would go along with him to
secure, first and foremost, his full co-operation.

Doreen walked back to the garden with
Cuaifeach following, and then Julia dismounted. Doreen wanted to give him a lump of sugar
for his efforts, but Julia said no, she wanted to
create the impression that they were doing him
a favour, not the other way round.

"But he was good, wasn't he?" the girl said,
looking with proud affection at her pony. "To
think it could be so easy!"

"Well," Julia replied, "we did cheat a little.
And you had better start practising your trot
and canter."

❋❋❋

The next two weeks saw some steady progress.
With Doreen as the proverbial carrot in front

of him, Cuaifeach learnt to trot and canter, halt and turn, go on and slow down. He was quick to learn and soon got to know the aids and commands. But he proved—not surprisingly— to be a very headstrong mount, with fixed ideas of his own. Exercises that he did not under- stand—such as lungeing—he simply would not take part in, and attempts to ride him away from Doreen failed as often as not, depending on his humour of the day. But though the gradual subjugation was not going according to plan, Julia stuck to her gentle and sympath- etic method. She did not want to use force to subdue him, partly because it was against her principles, but more importantly, because it could invite rebellion. She herself would have enough skill and strength to cope with that, but Doreen would not, when the time came for her to take over. She had only learnt to ride in the pony club on old dependable schoolmasters and the only way she would ever be able to control Cuaifeach would be by psychological means. He would have to obey because he wanted to, not because he was made to. However, for that to be achieved, a mental barrier would first have to be overcome. Julia hoped it would not prove insurmountable. Give it time, Eric would have said, with horses everything is a matter of time. You just have to be alert to it.

One morning Julia and Doreen decided to take Cuaifeach for a longer ride down the narrow road towards the point of Errislannan. He was getting bored with the beach, and on the road Doreen could go ahead on her bicycle. It was grey and damp as they set out. A cold mist had settled over the lake, and they passed it at a brisk pace to get warm. Then came a long uphill slope, and they slowed down out of consideration for Doreen, who relied on pedal power. Down in the dip, where the road followed the rocky sea-shore, they suddenly found themselves enveloped in thick white fog. Julia could no longer see Doreen on her bike; she could hardly see the pony's ears in front of her. At first she thought they had better turn back but then she became aware of a slight change in the stallion's body underneath her. It was so subtle, she might have missed it, if it hadn't been for the fact that this was exactly the sensation she had been waiting and hoping for: a sudden weakness, a lessening of resolve. A hint, ever so slight, but still, a hint of submission.

She gave the pony a pat of encouragement and told him to trot on. He obeyed tentatively—

but this time he was not being self-willed, merely unsure of himself. With as much reassurance and confidence as she could muster, Julia urged him on. The stallion listened attentively to her aids. It was obvious that he was lost and confused, not knowing quite where he was, unable to see his surroundings, only hearing the boom of the open sea that suggested nearby danger. He seemed to waver between his own sense of self-preservation which told him to retrace his steps and the instinct to turn to his rider for guidance. "Go on, Cuaifeach," Julia prompted him firmly, "I'll see you through. You know you can rely on me." And he did. He abandoned his misgivings and handed himself over to her. Weeks of building up his trust had not been for nothing.

"Are you all right, Julia?" came Doreen's voice through the fog.

"Yes, you go on," Julia called back in reply. "Wait for me at the crossroads."

Cuaifeach arrived there a different pony from the one who had left the cottage. For the first time in his life he had given himself in complete submission to his rider. And he had found the experience quite pleasurable; it made him feel, not only easy and relaxed, but also infinitely secure, a rare luxury for a headstrong nature like his.

Julia dismounted and took off her hard hat and the protective waistcoat that Eric had used to wear in races.

"What are you doing?" Doreen asked.

"Giving these to you. You're riding him back."

It was a risk, Julia knew. A risk but also a chance, Doreen's chance of gaining instant supremacy to compensate for her lack of experience. She had talked to the girl's parents who had said they were happy to leave all decisions to her, as they themselves understood so little about riding. It was a great responsibility. What if something went wrong? she asked herself with a sudden rush of fear, as she got on Doreen's bicycle to follow the equipage. But the strange thing was, she knew it would be all right, knew it just as she had known all along what had to be done with Cuaifeach. She couldn't explain it, the knowledge was just there.

Afterwards, as they sat by Julia's kitchen table having tea, Doreen's cheeks still flushed with the excitement of her success, Julia said to her: "There's one thing I have to confess."

"What?" Doreen wondered.

"I have never broken a horse before in my life."

"But..." the girl stammered..."but you knew it all...you seemed so sure."

"I only did what I thought Eric would have done. It felt almost as if he was there telling me what to do. I suppose when you've been with someone for so long...so close...you begin to function almost in the same way."

"Perhaps he was with us," Doreen said, her eyes round with emotion. She was silent for a moment, then she added: "I think he was with us today in the fog."

Julia smiled. "Perhaps he was."

9

A brand-new event had been added to the Conne-mara sporting calendar: a triathlon was to be held at Roc's Harbour just north of Roundstone at the end of August. The competition was open to young people under eighteen: you had to cycle a mile, swim a mile and ride a mile and the person with the best combined result would win a fabulous, as yet undisclosed, first prize.

The initiative attracted a huge amount of media attention, no doubt because it was headed by the famous sports celebrity Roc O'Neill. Addressing a press conference in the magnificent, marble-floored lobby of his leisure centre, the swimming star announced that it was high time someone introduced sound rules for competition in Connemara. These local people, he declared, smiling amiably at the assembled journalists and Johnny Tass, who had slipped in on the pretext of delivering mail, had a lot to learn. At local pony shows prizes were handed out like sweets from a bag to those who happened to be in favour with the judges. He found it disgraceful. His contest, by contrast, would be based on the proper Olympic principle that winning was all a matter of coming first.

Just as the leisure centre had encountered a certain amount of opposition amongst the local community, Roc's new project was greeted with a mixture of curiosity and suspicion. Many people were offended by his criticism of the existing fixtures. It was all very well to come up with a novel idea, but there was no need to be so scathing about things that everyone subscribed to and enjoyed. On one late night in O'Dowd's pub in Roundstone, the discussion became heated.

"He has no business coming here telling us how to run our shows," boomed a well-known hothead called Conor King. "It's all just a ruse anyway, to get publicity for that blasted leisure centre of his."

"I'd say so," another man agreed. "Didn't Johnny Tass tell me that any journalist who comes to write up the triathlon gets a free weekend at Roc's Harbour, with all the food and drink he can swallow."

"It's for the sake of the lad," suggested a third man. "To give him a chance to outshine our kids. Who else has a heated pool to practise his swimming, and an expert coach at hand?"

"He rides a real racing-bike," muttered man number four, "the most expensive model on the market."

"Sure enough he'll turn up with the winner of the Grand National for the riding class," someone else put in.

Everyone was in agreement that Roc O'Neill was a man who liked to win—what else would have driven him to acquire all those medals? Likewise he was a bad loser, as he had demonstrated at the Ballyconneely Show. It was significant that Dominic had not entered any of the other riding classes after that. His father probably would not let him compete unless victory was certain.

"It's not really fair, like," said one father of six who was held to be quite reasonable. "To use our kids like this, get them to enter a contest they have no chance of winning, just for the sake of glorifying his own brat."

"Let the lad do his own competing!" Conor

King shouted through the din. "Let him collect his blooming prize! But our kids should be kept out of it!"

"That's it, Jesus, that's it!" the others agreed. "Our kids will have no part in it."

But their children turned out to be quite easy-going about the whole thing. "Sure we'll go along," they told their angry fathers, "we'll go along for the crack. So what if we don't win—we'll still enjoy ourselves." And in the weeks leading up to the triathlon, the roads around Roundstone were full of children panting and heaving on their bikes, more heads than usual were seen bobbing in the sea on sunny days, and unsuspecting ponies were brought out to sandy tracks, mounted and made to gallop.

When Doreen sent in her entry-form, it was mainly because she thought this was something that Cuaifeach might enjoy. It would be a long time yet before he was ready for things like the pony club and normal riding classes, but here was something he was well able for: going forward in a straight line, going forward at speed.

Unfortunately, there was the business of her having to cycle and swim as well. The riding was the last class on the schedule, so unless she managed the other two, she would not be able to take part. Her friend Sheila was more favoured: she couldn't swim and didn't ride, but she could still take part in the first race for cyclists. Doreen went along to see her friend, asking for some "professional advice", and Sheila, like most self-styled experts, was flattered by the request and showed her all she knew about using the gears effectively and taking full advantage of the force of gravity. Then, after a moment of silent reflection, she offered Doreen the use of her own bike, which was much better and faster than Tom's old contraption.

Doreen protested at first. She knew what the bike meant to Sheila—almost as much as Cuaifeach meant to her—and besides, wasn't she going into the cycling race herself? The girl said it was all right, she could come along on Tom's bike. Doreen still hesitated, fearing that Sheila might regret it afterwards. "Come on," her friend told her, "We can't let Dominic have the whole field to himself. Someone has to stand up to him."

It surely won't be me, Doreen thought dejectedly. She might have had the shadow of a chance with Sheila's bike and Cuaifeach...but then there was the swimming to consider.

Swimming had never been part of the Connemara tradition. This might seem strange for a sea-faring people with constant access to water, but then, the sea was never regarded as a friend or an ally. It was an adversary— rough, cruel and unpredictable, negotiated only through the protective medium of a boat. It used to be an accepted fact that "the sea claimed its own" and little or no effort was made to save people drowning. While the concept of swimming for pleasure or sport gained ground in other countries, it was late to arrive in this part of the world—and, of course, the inclement climate did not help. And though Connemara children often watched intrepid holidaymakers take to the waves with a shriek, they themselves were less keen to follow.

Doreen's swimming so far had been limited to a few yards in shallow water on hot summer days at Gorteen. Now she would have to manage a whole mile, if she was to be admitted to the riding class. Never mind winning or even doing well—it was a matter of not getting herself disqualified.

Hearing of her dilemma, her father came up with a suggestion: Hadn't Ronan Kelly of Glinsk come back with a wife from Australia?

You knew what people were like down under, spent all day in the water like fish. He would have a word with Ronan. Sure the wife would be able to give Doreen a hint or two.

Mrs Kelly turned out to be a large, strong woman, somewhat on the stern side. This, Doreen's father explained, was on account of her being of German descent. She set to her appointed task with a commitment that far exceeded Doreen's own. Every day for a week she got the girl to plunge into the ice-cold waters off the deserted beach at Moyrus. The summer had been wet, with winds from the north, and the sea had hardly warmed up at all. Doreen was taught to dive and then to do a real Australian crawl, breathing calmly and rhythmically to enable her to go on for a full mile without getting too tired. She found that the harder she worked the less she felt the cold—it was as if she cocooned herself within the powerful movement, relaxed into her breathing, blotting out everything else. Her instructor was pleased with her progress and said she had a good natural aptitude. In Australia it was generally accepted that those who were good riders made good swimmers, and vice versa.

Julia, meanwhile, took the stallion for daily

gallops on Mannin Beach. Here Cuaifeach really came into his own. He went like a bullet amongst rocks and stray cattle, pounding the hard-packed sand with all the zest of a thoroughbred racehorse. The last week Doreen took over, shown by Julia how to ride jockey-style, stirrups short and her weight forward, out of the saddle. Here the girl's limited riding experience became an advantage: she had no problem adjusting to the different technique.

The last day of training came and Doreen took her pony for a last spin on the beach. All went well. She didn't push Cuaifeach at all, just let him go along comfortably at his own pace, reserving his strength for the big day. On her way back, a fast bicycle whizzed past her on the main road, then stopped and waited. As the rider turned round to face her, she recognised him as Dominic O'Neill. He watched Cuaifeach intently.

"Is this the stallion everyone is talking about?" he asked in his drawling big city accent, so unlike the tone of Connemara.

Doreen halted. The edge of resentment in his voice revealed that what he had heard was not to his liking. She, too, was aware of the gossip. People in Connemara were pinning their hopes on Cuaifeach, looking to him—and her!—to provide a serious challenge to the O'Neills. She had tried to turn a deaf ear; she was not going into this contest with a view to winning. All she wanted was a good day out for herself and her pony.

"It's Cuaifeach," she replied, "if that's what you mean."

Dominic still had his eyes on the pony, who was standing there quiet and thoughtful, his energy spent. Then he said condescendingly: "He looks like a real slug."

"He's tired out," the girl informed him. "So would you be, if you'd been galloping along Mannin Beach like a streak of lightning."

"Streak of lightning?" Dominic sneered. "He isn't even sweating!"

"And I'll tell you why," said Doreen, "it's because he's the fittest pony in Connemara. A mile will be nothing to him."

"Oh?" Dominic seemed surprised. "You're thinking of taking him along to the triathlon?"

"Of course," Doreen replied, sounding a little more haughty than she intended. "Why wouldn't I?"

"It's just that my Dad's been talking about banning stallions from the race," Dominic drawled casually.

"What?" Doreen exclaimed, shattered. "Why

would he be doing that?"

The boy shrugged. "He says they are too dangerous to have around. He doesn't want any accidents. You know, insurance and all that."

The sight of his spiteful face was enough to make her speechless. But then Doreen pulled herself up in the saddle and said slowly: "I had heard that you were desperate to win, Dominic. But I hadn't realised that you were quite so afraid of losing."

With that she trotted off, annoyed, not only with Dominic but also with herself, for allowing herself to be drawn into his game. And deep inside she felt a burning sensation of something that she had so far managed to hold back, knowing it would do her no good. It was the seething, consuming desire to see Dominic O'Neill well and truly beaten.

❋❋❋

Whether Dominic's threat was just a hoax to unsettle her or whether Roc thought the better of the idea and scrapped it, there was no more mention of stallions being banned from the triathlon, and Doreen turned up for the first race as if nothing had happened, got her number and tied it around her waist. Her brother Tom was there, too, with his new bike. Like Sheila and many of the other cyclists, he had come along for this race only, with no plans to enter the other two.

More than forty young cyclists had turned up at the starting-point—the broad bit of road outside Roundstone church—and a sizeable crowd, including, of course, all the parents and siblings, were there to see them off. With so many riders, and such a narrow road ahead of them, it was mainly a matter of getting off to a good start and then finding a gap to get through. A group of a dozen or so riders broke away at an early stage. Thanks to Sheila's bike and instructions, Doreen was amongst these, as were Tom and Dominic. They proceeded in a light drizzle, with Roc's white Mercedes in front to warn oncoming traffic, past hay-meadows lush and green from the plentiful rain and the odd surprised donkey taking to the verge in alarm. The front riders pedalled hard where the road led gently uphill. Doreen, the only girl amongst them, found it hard to keep up with the boys and fell back a little. Then on the straight she managed to overtake a couple of them again. She arrived at the finish, just by the entrance to Roc's Harbour, in ninth place.

Tom had done well—he came in third—whereas poor Sheila ended up well back in the field. Dominic was seventh—he wasn't the only one with a racing-bike. The boy who won came from far away and none of the others knew him.

Quite a few of the onlookers faced a moral dilemma that morning, as the swimming class coincided with Sunday Mass. This was a bit of bad planning on Roc's side, but then, he wasn't very religious. Some had already solved the problem by going to Mass on Saturday evening, others abstained altogether, hoping to be forgiven. After all, it was not every day that you got a chance to see for yourself the spectacular new leisure centre from inside.

The giant Roc pool was housed separately from the other structures down by the shore. The whole interior was lined with sea-green ceramic tiles; the long wall facing the sea had sliding glass panels and a terrace outside, so that on good days you could sunbathe by the poolside. On the back wall splendid pillars of Connemara marble surrounded the entrance to the changing-rooms, and at one end was a bar with comfortable rattan furniture. The opposite wall was all but covered by a huge

sea-water aquarium, which gave the illusion
that you were actually looking into the ocean.
Someone remarked that the whole thing was
like a James Bond movie.

Of the many contenders in the cycling race,
all except fourteen pulled out when it came to
the swimming. Johnny Tass informed Doreen
that of these only half had brought ponies:
these were the ones she had to watch. He gave
her a quick run-down on them as they were
ranked after the cycling: in the lead was a
tough, wiry little boy called Eamonn from East
Galway. He had a very fast pony, Johnny said,
he hunted with the Galway Blazers, and
everyone knew what they were like: went like
the clappers regardless of anything standing
in their way. Developed hearts like lions they
did, those hunting kids.

"Good," said Doreen. "He may win, so."

Dominic was in second place, followed by
Doreen and a girl called Barbara. She was the
daughter of a Clifden solicitor and went to
boarding-school in Dublin during term-time.
With her beautiful dappled grey pony she was
the star of the pony club and had won
numerous ridden show classes. Moreover, she
was a strong swimmer and had represented
her school in some national tournament. Down

the line were the Mannion brothers, whose
father had the trekking centre at Rosmuc.
Their ponies did not look very speedy and they
had not done too well in the cycling but you
never knew. Finally there was a small,
determined-looking girl who had brought her
pony, a smart Welsh palomino, all the way
from Wicklow to her holiday home near
Moyard. She was younger than the others, and
with her smaller bike had been one of the last
in the cycling. Chances were it would be the
same with her pony.

"If you could only get ahead of the first two,"
Johnny said, "you'd be in a much better
position for the riding."

"And how could I?" said Doreen. "You know
as well as I do that Dominic will win this class."

The swimmers took up their positions.
Doreen looked down at the shimmering green
tiles, trying to remember what Mrs Kelly had
taught her about starting and turning in a pool:
she had only ever swum in the sea. At least it
would be warmer than Moyrus, she thought;
all the adverts for the leisure centre made
much of the "Mediterranean water temperature". But when the starting-shot went and she
dived in, she was startled to find that the
Mediterranean was every bit as cold as the

Atlantic.

Without further reflection, Doreen started to crawl, concentrating on her breathing and the steady, vigorous movement. Soon she was oblivious of everything else, of the yelping protests from Dominic that the heating system had failed and of his father's curt command to shut up and get on with it. She was equally unaware of the cheering and shouting, dominated by Mrs Kelly's deep voice, and of the sudden commotion at the opposite end of the pool.

It was Eamonn from East Galway who had got into trouble. He was not a very good swimmer but, thinking he could cope, had jumped in, determined to have a go. After the first couple of lengths he had become very tired, but he gritted his teeth and continued, as he would in the hunting field, where there was no such thing as opting out. Bravely he struggled on, until the moment came when he was overcome by muscle fatigue. He felt himself going down, down, unable to summon the strength to keep himself afloat or even call for help. The first one alerted to his plight was Mrs Kelly: without a moment's hesitation she jumped in, fully dressed, and rescued him. By then he was already in a bad way and had to be seen by the doctor on standby.

"Just like these hunting kids," said Seamus Lee, shaking his head. "Leap in at the deep end, shut your eyes and hope for the best. It didn't work this time."

Through all this Doreen swam and swam, back and forth, length after length after length, until she felt a hand grab hers at the end of the pool. It was one of the stewards.

"You can stop now," he said, "you finished your mile three lengths ago."

Exhausted, she climbed out and shook her head to get the water out of her ears. "Who won?" she asked the steward.

"The girl over there," he said, indicating Barbara, who was standing by the poolside looking unconcerned, as if she had known all along that victory was hers. She usually kept aloof and did not mix with the local children, so that there were those who called her a snob. But Doreen felt she liked her better now for having got the better of the young O'Neill.

"You were second," the steward told her.

Second! Where, then, was Dominic? Doreen looked around to see the Mannion brothers and the young girl from Wicklow fighting for third place. Dominic was still in the pool, making his way towards the end where his father was

waiting, a furious look on his face. The boy
grimaced, as if he was in severe pain. "Am I
finished?" he panted.

"About time, too," Roc snapped. "What the
hell do you think you're doing?"

"I got cramp," Dominic wailed, on the verge
of tears. "It's the cold water, I've never swum
in cold water before."

Roc just turned and walked away from him.

❋❋❋

Gorteen Beach had been converted into a racecourse. Gone were the sunbathers, the
swimmers and the windsurfers, replaced by a
motley crowd of racegoers, tourists in jeans and
sunglasses, local people in Sunday clothes, men
in suits, women in dresses and high heels, not
the best footwear for the deep sand. A book-
maker had set up his blackboard and was
offering bets, though not with much success,
as he was a stranger to the area and few people
trusted him. A professional racing commentator brought all the way from the Curragh was
introducing the contestants over crackling
loudspeakers. There were stalls selling soft
drinks and chocolate, and a white trailer had
been towed in by a tractor to serve hamburgers

and chips.

"It's just like it used to be," sighed the old people nostalgically looking back to the golden era of pony racing in the first half of this century. Those were the days when meetings were held on each decent beach and racing ponies became legends in their own lifetime. There was the celebrated Cannon Ball, foundation stallion and number one in the stud book, who won more races than any other pony. When he died, he was waked for three days, and he was buried standing up, facing the Oughterard racecourse. But nowadays pony racing had more or less died out. And whatever people thought about Roc O'Neill, they were grateful to him for bringing back this spectacular pleasure.

The beach was only half a mile long so the riders were to turn round a post at the far end and come back to finish where they started. Two red-and-white posts marked the goal. Now they had a string stretched between them to serve as the starting-line.

After Eamonn's disqualification in the swimming class, the number of riders had been reduced to six: they were Barbara on her beautiful show pony, Dominic on Rosie, the O'Briens' flighty chestnut mare, Doreen on

Cuaifeach, the Mannion brothers on their sturdy trekking ponies and the young girl from Wicklow on her fiery small palomino, which was already pawing the ground impatiently, rearing to go.

Cuaifeach took it all in with a level head, but then, he was never excited when he was supposed to, only when it was least expected—that was his charm and, perhaps, his problem. He was surrounded by well-wishers. Christy, remembering the old days, was so worked up he could hardly stand still. Doreen's parents were looking at their daughter in some wonderment, as parents do when their children achieve something well beyond their own capabilities. Tom was there, too, and Julia, who was patting the stallion and talking to the young jockey:

"Remember you're out to have a good time. Don't worry about winning, don't push him too hard. Let him know he is here to enjoy himself; he's too young for any serious competing."

The riders lined up their mounts and the string was cut. Rosie was off in a flash—of all the participating ponies, she was no doubt the one most like a racehorse in build and temperament. Barbara's well-schooled gelding took up the pursuit, then came the Mannion brothers, followed by Cuaifeach. The girl from Wicklow was already in trouble: her pony was playing up, refusing to pass the big rocks at the beginning of the track. When she whipped him furiously, he bucked her off into the water. She got on again and continued, but was by then well behind the others.

Cuaifeach seemed to have taken to heart Julia's words about enjoying himself. He made no effort at all, just cantered along leisurely as if he didn't have a care in the world. If he could, he would have whistled, or hummed a tune. His attention wandered from one thing to another: the crowds, the other ponies, the translucent light over the blue-green lagoon, as the sun unexpectedly broke through the cloud.

Rosie was leading by about five lengths when she approached the turning-post. Roc was watching, elated, through binoculars. Dominic only had to win this race to take home the first prize. He did not realise that his son was completely out of control. No way was he able to stop the mare and turn her round. She galloped on, up the sand-dunes at the far end and disappeared out of sight.

Barbara's super-conditioned animal was beginning to feel the strain of his surplus weight. He was puffing like a pair of bellows but obliged at the turning-post and set off towards the goal in a leading position, soon, however, to be overtaken by the Mannion brothers, who did all their running side by side. Cuaifeach, too, turned well and was gaining ground though he still seemed convinced that the outing was for pleasure only. He met the Wicklow pony, still on its way to the turning-post. Then there was a thunder of hooves coming up behind him: Dominic had at length managed to point Rosie's nose in the right direction and was going hell for leather to make up for lost time. In an instant the penny dropped for Cuaifeach: He was in a race. A race! Yippee!

Doreen leant further forward over the pony's neck and dug her heels in. Cuaifeach got the message and lengthened his stride. In no time at all he had passed out the flagging show pony and the two Mannions; she just saw them flash past to the left and right. Now she was in the lead! Rosie was getting closer but so were the goal-posts. If she could only keep him going at this pace for another hundred yards...

The rhythm of the horse became her own, her arms moved with his neck, her body with his, as if they were fused together into one, going faster and faster. This is my moment! the girl thought euphorically. Win or lose, this is it, all I ever dreamt of!

"And it is Cuaifeach!" came the commentator's excited voice from the loudspeakers. "It is Cuaifeach, from Rosie, as they race for home! And it is Cuaifeach still in the lead..."

The crowd was getting riotous. At one end were Roc and the O'Briens and those employees from the leisure centre who had been drafted in to act as stewards. "Faster, Dominic!" Roc bellowed furiously, "faster!" "Go on, Rosie!" shouted the O'Briens. "For Chrissake, go on!"

Cuaifeach's supporters formed a larger and noisier choir. "Good girl!" cried Christy until his old man's voice cracked, "good girl!" "Come on, Doreen!" shouted her father, Julia and Sheila, while the rest, headed by Johnny Tass, contented themselves with roaring: "Cuaifeach, Cuaifeach!" in a steady rhythm.

Rosie was now so close that Doreen could see her from the corner of her eye. Dominic whipped her frantically. But they were only a few strides from home. He wouldn't make it, he wouldn't!

"And it is Cuaifeach..." called the commentator. "Cuaifeach from Rosie..."

The crowd was in raptures.

Then the chipper blew up.

It had been parked quite near the finish, where most of the crowds were, but no one had been buying chips while the race was in progress. Preparing for a rush once it was over, the chipper man had turned the burner up to keep the oil hot. When nothing happened, he bent down to adjust the old-fashioned attachment of the gas cylinder. The next thing he was aware of was a loud bang, and the startled faces of bystanders, as he came hurtling out the door, his face black, most of his hair missing. Flames were leaping from the trough of burning oil, a cloud of black smoke came billowing out of the chimney.

All the local men rushed to help put out the fire. In Connemara, where there is no ready access to fire engines, everyone acts as a fireman whenever the need arises. The spare gas canister was dragged away to prevent a major disaster. A fire blanket was located and used to smother the flames. Miraculously, no one was injured.

At the moment of the explosion, the two contenders for the first prize had been only feet away from the goal-posts. Both ponies, naturally, responded: Cuaifeach by cautiously arresting his stride, Rosie by acting as if a mortar bomb had been detonated underneath her belly: She literally flew in the air, and then lunged forward, throwing Dominic as she did so. But when she landed, all four feet were the other side of the finishing-line. Dominic, likewise, hit home on all fours—Cuaifeach had to swerve to avoid trampling him.

Who had won? Nobody knew, no one had been looking—all gazes had automatically turned to the exploding chipper. Only after the panic was over did people turn their minds back to the race, asking each other: Who was the winner?

Roc took the microphone from the commentator, who looked as though he regretted having come to Connemara at all, and announced that the stewards and judges would have a meeting to determine the outcome of the triathlon. The result would be declared officially in the lobby of the leisure centre at six o'clock.

People were already gathering around Doreen, congratulating her, hailing Cuaifeach as a hero. But the O'Neill camp, too, seemed to be celebrating victory.

At six the lobby was crammed. Press, friends, guests and employees of Roc O'Neill were admitted first, so many of the locals had to throng by the open door. It was, someone remarked, like church at a good funeral. Roc and the three judges—all, needless to say, old cronies of his from the world of sport—appeared on a specially erected podium at one end. The six contenders were called up, and Roc grabbed a microphone.

"I am speaking on behalf of the judges," he began. "They've had a hard decision to make."

"As long as you didn't make it for them!" came a voice from the floor.

Roc ignored the remark. "However, after much deliberation, with the help of the stewards and with all relevant factors considered, they have arrived at a unanimous verdict."

"The stewards all work for him!" Conor King pointed out to the others. "They shouldn't have any say in this!"

With a grand gesture Roc handed over the mike to one of the judges, who announced, somewhat deprecatingly, it seemed, that they had agreed to follow the Olympic rule that the first one over the finishing-line was the winner. The first prize, a trip for two to Disneyland in Florida—"

Here he paused, expecting applause, but it did not materialise, so he continued: "This prize has been awarded to Dominic O'Neill."

Roc beamed. His friends and employees clapped obligingly, as Dominic stepped forward to receive a large silver cup and an envelope from the other judges. But the crowd were not impressed. "Boo!" they shouted. "This is cheating! Boo!"

"It will sure be a nice break for Roc!" someone commented loudly.

"The second prize," the judge went on, "is one hundred pounds. The winner is Doreen Joyce. All the prizes, incidentally, have been kindly donated by our generous host, Roc O'Neill—"

"Roc O'Bottom, if you ask me!" called Seamus Lee.

The crowd burst into peals of laughter. Roc's affable smile faded. He was not afraid of making himself unpopular, he had had more than his fill of adulation, but, like most such people, he drew the line at being ridiculed. He quickly took the microphone from the judge.

"We do realise," he said placatingly, "that there was a bit of a misadventure—"

"The worst misadventure here is yerself!" roared Conor King, who had got up to stand on a chair. "Go back to Dublin! Take the lad and yer blooming Olympic rules with you!

We've had enough of ye!"

Roc looked down at the sea of faces in front of him and read the resentment and indignation written on many of them. This he had not expected. There were the journalists to consider as well. They were scribbling away madly on their notepads.

"In the circumstances," he said in a loud, authoritative voice, "I think the best bet would be to award two first prizes. I shall donate another trip to Disneyland. Doreen—where are you, my girl?"

She stepped forward reluctantly. Roc snatched the envelope from Dominic's hand and held it out to her.

"Here is your travel voucher. I hope you'll enjoy your trip."

Doreen did not take it. "Sorry now," she said quietly, "but I'd rather hold on to my second prize, if you don't mind."

"What?" Roc said, disconcerted. "Why do you say that? Don't you want to go to Disneyland?"

"I'd rather have the money," Doreen said simply. "It's expensive enough to keep a stallion, and my savings have run out."

Roc smiled broadly in relief. He had feared that the girl would push the issue further. "In that case," he said magnanimously, "I am not one to go back on my word. The ticket to Disneyland may be exchanged against cash. Five hundred pounds. How is that?"

"All right with me," said Doreen.

"A big hand!" Roc commanded, "for the two winners!"

But the applause remained scattered until he took the trophy Dominic was holding and ceremoniously presented it to Doreen.

"Three cheers for Cuaifeach!" Johnny Tass shouted. "Hip, hip, hurrah!"

The cheering continued while the remaining prizes were handed out, to Barbara, the Mannions and the Wicklow girl respectively. Then, as the contenders left the podium, Dominic approached Doreen.

"I'm sorry about all this," he said, looking rather embarrassed. "I think you should have won outright."

"Never mind," Doreen said, smiling. "To me winning is not just a matter of coming first."

From the loudspeakers Roc's voice announced that there would be a free drink for everyone in the bar.

That was enough for them to forgive him.

The Freedom of the Bens

10

utumn was creeping in over the Twelve Bens. The bright green fronds of the fern had turned russet, the grass of the bogs was losing its summer freshness. Although the sun was shining bright and warm as in mid-summer, the landscape was slowly going to rest. Growth was stagnating, the water of the streams was no longer rushing towards the sea. Animals moved languidly with no goal in sight; birds stayed in one place, the bustle of spring forgotten.

Doreen held in her pony and looked out over a broad valley, desolate stretches of bog and stone without any sign of human habitation. Dreamily she continued along the stony track. This was how she had imagined life with Cuaifeach: days of exploring unknown territory, the two of them getting to know the world, closely bonded by love and friendship. The day lay before them wide open, inviting them to partake of fun and adventure, freedom of movement and brand-new horizons.

Descending into the valley, she suddenly had the impression that space had taken over from time. Tomorrow and its worrisome clouds no longer existed. She and her pony were here and now. They were together and fulfilled and nothing else mattered.

She had ridden from Inishnee in the early hours of the morning, on deserted roads where the only sound to be heard was the clickety-click of Cuaifeach's new shoes. You could tell he was proud of them, or of the noise they made, for he flicked his feet self-consciously and looked around for spectators, as always when he was showing off. But there was no one to witness his tap-dancing. At this time of a September morning Connemara was fast asleep.

They had gone past Toombeola and then through Ballinahinch. The forest was a bit spooky with its dark shadows and all its unfamiliar sounds, creaking of boughs, sighing of treetops. Neither Doreen nor her pony were used to being among so many trees. It was a relief to get out on the main road and then branch off into the wide open spaces of the Bens. Stark and exposed, they often made strangers uneasy, but those who knew them found peace and security in their open embrace. It was like being welcomed into an infinite home.

Julia had tipped Doreen off about this road as she had come up here to paint. To begin with it led steeply uphill past the odd stone cottage and a few modern bungalows with neatly tended gardens. Then it meandered between the foothills, through the broad valley. Where the road ended a grassy track lead alongside a stream to an abandoned homestead.

As they proceeded through the valley, Cuaifeach became restive and less attentive, he kept looking searchingly around him, now and then emitting a resounding stallion cry. It was as if the wilderness surrounding them had touched some primitive nerve inside him. Doreen had to keep reminding him that she was there, too. Theirs was a joint adventure; it wasn't as if he was out on his own.

By the time they reached the homestead, the sun was high in the sky. The grey, half-ruined buildings nestled comfortably under the mountains, like a natural part of the landscape: you almost expected a fairy to come walking out the door. In the old pens the grass was high, the soil still dry and healthy.

They were both ready for a rest. Doreen took off Cuaifeach's saddle and replaced the bridle with the head-collar she had tied round her waist. Then she led him down to the stream for a long draught of rippling, crystal-clear water. Her own refreshment she had brought with sandwiches in a small rucksack. Before sitting down to eat, she tied the pony to the remains of an old donkey-cart left inside a pen.

The sun was lovely, the stillness complete. She opened her food parcel and, leaning against a warm granite slab, enjoyed her sandwiches seasoned by the scent of dry grass and wild flowers. A stoat came out from behind an outhouse and looked at her, surprised but not startled. She threw him a piece of bread, but he did not take it.

Hearing a snort from Cuaifeach, she turned round and saw him sniffing furiously at a heap of fresh manure. He pawed the ground and looked darkly around. "Stallion dung!" he seemed to be muttering. "Where is that scoundrel?"

"Don't be silly!" she called out to him. "It's your own dung. You left it there a minute ago!"

Cuaifeach, apparently having reached the same conclusion, sheepishly withdrew and started to graze. But he remained unsettled and kept scanning the horizon, whinnying anxiously as if he was afraid of missing something.

"You better get some rest while you can," Doreen advised him. "We have a long way to go home."

She closed her eyes, listening to the singing of the stream, breathing in the crisp air of September. This, she thought, is how I imagine paradise. She wanted to savour the moment, make it last for as long as possible, conserve it for future recollection. Soon, much too soon, it would be over. Winter would set in.

But her moment was cut short. For on the ridge over to the east a herd of seven mares had appeared, summoned by the mating call of the stallion. He looked up and saw them, standing out against the blue autumn sky. They were small and shaggy, but they were mares, and he wasn't fussy. Cuaifeach reared up, giving a violent tug with his head. The decayed wood of the cart splintered in all directions. The next instant he was off, up the slope, towards the mares, towards the allure of utter freedom.

Doreen ran after him, frantically calling his name. But before she even started to climb the slope, he was gone over the ridge with the mares. She could hear them gallop down the other side and knew she did not stand a chance of catching up with them.

"Cuaifeach!" she cried, though she might as well have called on the grey mountains. "Oh Cuaifeach, how could you? How could you do this to me?"

The thunder of hooves came closer and then she saw them again up on the crest. With Cuaifeach in the lead they came running towards her. For a hopeful moment she thought he was coming back, but not at all, they galloped past her and around in a huge circle. Her pony looked back at her a couple of times, tossing his head proudly, showing off as usual. This was his herd, he seemed to say, his own little harem. Wasn't he great to have found them?

They disappeared once more, and all Doreen could do was climb the ridge to see where they had gone. It was a steep ascent and she was hot and out of breath by the time she reached the top. The herd of ponies was still on the move. They were down in a small valley before her. Down there was a small grey cottage with a fenced-in pen and a large tumbledown shed. At first she thought it was another deserted farm, it looked so rundown and untended. But then she saw a thin wisp of smoke rising from the chimney and a sheepdog in front of the house. Someone was there, someone who might be able to help her.

It took her the better part of an hour to find her way down the rough hillside. The ponies galloped on, now in, now out of sight. As she came closer to the cottage, she saw two men moving in the enclosure, shouting to each other, pointing at the ponies. Then one of them rattled a bucket in his hand. The herd appeared from nowhere, the mares now in the lead, Cuaifeach following. They hurtled themselves down the mountain, into the pen, where all of them except Cuaifeach tried to get their heads into the bucket at once.

The man with the bucket led them, the other one drove them from behind into the big shed. A moment later, the mares were let out again at the other end, but Cuaifeach, whinnying desperately, remained inside.

Thanks be to God! Doreen thought, as she

rushed up to the man, who was just pulling a rusty bolt across the door of the shed. Now she recognised him. It was Joe Will. His cousin Tom Samuel was busy chasing the mares off, up the hill.

"Thank you!" she cried. "Oh, thanks a million! He ran away from me, and I was afraid I'd never be able to catch him again!"

Joe Will gave her a surly look from under the peak of a grimy cap. "Is the horse yours?" he asked, loud and abrupt as usual.

Before she had time to answer, Tom Samuel chipped in: "Sure you remember, he was at Maam Cross. They knocked ours and passed hers."

He sounded so indignant that Doreen had a feeling they somehow held her responsible for this.

"Don't you know," Joe Will said to her in a tone not without aggression, "stallions aren't allowed on the mountain."

"Well of course," Doreen stammered, "but he ran away...I couldn't help it."

Joe, sucking one of his few remaining molars, exchanged a glance with his cousin. Then they joined forces, telling her gruffly that this was awkward, like. For all they knew, her horse could have got all their mares into foal.

Doreen assured them that there was no question of that. She had seen them, they had only been galloping together for a short while. But the cousins did not believe her. They said they would not release the stallion unless her father wrote a note for the Society admitting that their stallion had been loose on the mountain.

"Of course we will," Doreen promised. "Anything you say. Only please let me have my pony back."

Joe Will was standing with his back against the door of the shed, where Cuiafeach could still be heard lamenting the departure of his harem. "Not until we have the note," he said doggedly. "From yer Dad."

"And how shall I get home?" Doreen asked. "I'm a long way from home. You know that."

Tom Samuel muttered that she should have thought about that before setting out. Joe Will said she could walk, that's what they had to do all the time, it wouldn't kill her.

With a heavy heart, Doreen scrambled back over the mountain to the homestead where she had left her things, including Julia's saddle. She thought of all the concerns and worries she had had for Cuaifeach in the past year and asked herself whether the moments of joy she had experienced inbetween really outweighed them. The problem was that the good times did not last—they never did. Perhaps it was a fact of life that the minute all was well in the world, some force moved in to destroy it. It was the same thing at home. After all the sadness, they had once more become a happy family: since her father came back, her mother's depression had vanished like magic, the cottage had filled with joy and laughter, there was warmth and security for everyone. And yet her parents weren't satisfied, they were reaching out for other things, different things, that meant giving up all that they had...Oh, did life really have to be like that?

She forgot that she had vowed to banish all these thoughts for today. This was to have been a memorable day of happy, carefree adventure for her and Cuaifeach—the last one, perhaps, that they would ever have.

And now, thanks to him, they didn't even have that.

While she gathered up her belongings, wondering whether she'd be able to carry the heavy saddle all the way back, she heard the distant spinning of a car engine cut through the early evening silence. She looked up towards the road and saw a white car driving through the valley. It was Julia's car! There, at least, was someone who had never let her down. Not yet, anyway. She went up the track to meet her.

"How did you find me?" she asked.

"Tom told me you'd gone riding in the Bens. And ponies leave traces, you know. Especially when they wear shoes."

She reached into the car and took out a painting.

"I went over to Inishnee," she said, "to give you this."

The picture was of Cuaifeach running valiantly into the wind. Behind him, in diminished perspective, was a Connemara landscape reminiscent of the Bens. He looked just the way he had when he was with the mares on the mountain. Doreen looked away.

"Don't you like it?" Julia asked.

"I've seen all I want of that horse," Doreen said bitterly. "I thought I could trust him, but I was wrong."

And out came the story of his running away, and being caught and held to ransom by Joe Will and Tom Samuel.

"But you can't hold that against him," Julia protested. "He can't help being a stallion; he was only following his nature."

"It seems to me," Doreen burst out vehemently, "that everyone feels free to just follow their nature. Everyone except me, that is. I just have to do as I'm told."

"Doreen," Julia said softly, "what really is the matter?"

The sympathy in her voice brought tears to Doreen's eyes, but she said nothing.

"Please, Doreen," Julia entreated her. "Tell me about it. Whatever it is, you know you can talk to me."

"It's my Mam and Dad," Doreen began, stifling a sob. "They want to go and live in London. And Tom and I are to go with them."

"Has this come on suddenly?" Julia asked. It was the first she had heard of the family emigrating.

Doreen nodded. "Dad had a letter from his old boss, offering him his job back. With a big raise, and a nice flat to go with it. Mam says she won't let him go without her this time, and she is dead keen anyway, says she's had enough of carrying turf and heating water. Now she wants to live in comfort, with a bathroom and central heating."

"And Tom?" Julia asked. "What does he think about it?"

"Oh, he's all set. He wants to go to technical college in London. But no one has asked me what I want. I don't want to go anywhere. I want to stay here."

Julia was silent for a while. Then she said slowly: "I had to sacrifice a lot for Eric. His career always had to come first. And yet, don't you think I would have preferred that to losing him? If you are lucky enough to have people you love, people you belong with, you sometimes have to do things for their sake, even if it isn't what you yourself want to do. It's what love is all about."

"But Mam and Dad aren't the only ones I belong with," Doreen argued. "There's Cuaifeach. What will become of him? He depends on me, even more than Mam and Dad."

"You should have reminded him of that," Julia said smiling, "when he took off up the mountain."

"But that was my fault," Doreen retorted, "for not tying him up properly."

She picked up Julia's painting and looked thoughtfully at the portrait of her stallion. Somehow the artist had captured the very essence of his being: the pony born of a fairy-wind, careering into life, meeting it head-on, as if it were a refreshing westerly breeze.

"I do love Cuaifeach," she said gently. "I only ever wanted to do what was best for him. But from his point of view, nothing I did was right. I locked him up, I packed him off to Molly to get kicked, I've been scheming for months to have him castrated. Julia, if you had only seen what he was like running free with those mares! He was so delighted, it was like stars shining all over him. Racing at Gorteen was nothing by comparison."

"Well you couldn't have let him loose on the mountain," Julia reminded her. "That's against the law."

"I just feel I'm no good to him. Perhaps the best thing I can do is to go away and leave him. See if someone will take him for me."

Julia did not say anything for a long while. When, at length, she spoke, the words came out tentatively, as if an idea was just forming in her mind. "I've been offered a lease," she said, "of the cottage at Errislannan. A bit of land goes with it. If I stayed for the winter, Cuaifeach could run there with a couple of mares. I could carry on with his training. That would give him the best of both worlds. And you would know he was in good hands. If you have to go to England."

"You think I should go?" Doreen asked.

"If it's what your parents want, I can't see that you have any choice."

"Will you stay, for sure?"

"Up till now I was undecided," Julia told her. "But perhaps this is reason enough to go ahead. It will give me something to live for. And Cuaifeach will still be yours, he will always be there for you."

"Oh Julia," Doreen said, "I shall have your painting with me always. It will hang over my bed, to remind me of the best two friends I ever had in this world."

They collected her things and started to drive back on the narrow winding road. About halfway through the valley they had to stop. A red van was coming towards them. It was Sean and Roisin Joyce.

She and her father met on the road. "Are you all right?" was the first thing he said. "Where is Cuaifeach?"

"Oh Dad," she cried, "he ran away from me on the mountain, and now Joe Will and Tom Samuel have got him, and they won't let him go unless you write a note to say he's been with their mares."

"Well isn't it just like those rascals," her father muttered. "They've had that scruffy little colt of theirs running with the mares all summer. We were just wondering what trick they would be up to, to get papers for the foals."

"But you have to give them the note," Doreen insisted, "or they won't give Cuaifeach back."

"I'll give him a note all right," said Sean Joyce. "A note to say Cuaifeach was on the mountain in September. Then, when the foals arrive three months early, they'll have some explaining to do."

Only then did it occur to Doreen to ask her parents what brought them to the Bens.

"We were looking for you, sure," said her mother. "When you didn't come back in time, we got worried. You could have had a fall. Or else we thought..."

Her father gave a wry smile. "Mam was convinced you'd run away from home."

"Me?" said Doreen offended. "Do you think I'm as bad as Cuaifeach?"

Her mother hugged her. "You had us real worried. We realised, of course, that you didn't want to go to England, and we know how you love that horse. But never mind. It doesn't matter now."

"It's lovely up here," her father said to Julia.

"I'm glad we came. It helped us, somehow, to get things into perspective."

"We were standing up there," Doreen's mother said, pointing to one of the hills, "looking out over the valley, searching for Doreen. We saw the greatness of it all, the freedom and the peace...and we said to each other, do we really want to give this up for a flat with central heating?"

Doreen looked unsurely at her parents, from one to the other.

"I thought of the traffic and the noise and the dirt in London," her father went on, "and I said to Roisin, perhaps our Doreen's the one's got it right. After all, isn't the main thing in life that, when you wake up in the morning, you are in the one place you want to be?"

"With your loved ones around you," her mother added, not forgetting her heartache of the previous winter.

"You're not going?" Doreen asked, in a voice so low it hardly carried.

"We're not," her father said. "Work or no work, we're staying."

"We're both agreed," her mother concluded, "that there's nothing in the world can make up for what we have in Connemara."

Doreen's father was watching something

moving in the foothills far away to the east. The others followed his gaze and saw a pony picking its way confidently amongst the rocks, skilfully avoiding steep declines and boggy patches.

"If it isn't Cuaifeach!" Sean Joyce exclaimed.

"He must have broken out of his shed," Doreen said vaguely, as if she couldn't quite believe it.

"He's come looking for you," Julia stated.

The stallion had now reached the valley and was galloping towards them at great speed. Doreen's eyes glittered tenderly as she watched her pony, the strong muscular body moving in the rhythm she knew so well, the smooth bay coat glistening in the autumn sunshine, the wild black mane streaming around his head.

"That horse," she said, feeling a big lump in her throat. "Whatever made me think I could live without him?"

Rosie's Century

by

ANN CARROLL

A letter from the past, a set of clues, the threat of murder – these bring Rosie back to the gas-lit streets of Dublin 1900 for another great adventure.

It is April and Queen Victoria is about
to visit the city.

Rosie has learnt nothing in school about this event
and she's amazed at the Dubliners' enthusiasm
for the queen.

But beneath the holiday atmosphere evil lurks . . .

ISBN 1 85371 972 2

£4.99

Rosie's Century by **Ann Carroll**
available from Poolbeg,
the *Irish* for bestsellers

Rosie's Gift

by

ANN CARROLL

*What was it like to be a skivvy in 1870, slaving away in
a big house at everyone's beck and call?*

For time-traveller Rosie McGrath – used to the
dishwasher and central heating of modern times –
it is a horrible shock. But she must suffer on if she
wants to save her ancestor Joseph and foil the
plans of a powerful enemy!

ISBN 1 85371 875 0

£4.99

Rosie's Gift by **Ann Carroll**
available from Poolbeg,
the *Irish* for bestsellers

Rosie's Troubles

by

ANN CARROLL

Dublin in 1920 was a dangerous, violent city.
A twelve-year-old girl on her own could easily
disappear without trace.

Was Catherine Dalton caught up in the mayhem
of Croke Park on bloody Sunday? Was she murdered
and secretly buried?

Rosie's gran still wonders what happened to her
best friend. To find out, Rosie must travel
once more to the past, putting her own life
and future at risk.

ISBN 1 85371 681 2

£4.99

Rosie's Troubles by **Ann Carroll**
available from Poolbeg,
the *Irish* for bestsellers

Rosie's Quest

by

ANN CARROLL

Dublin, Friday the 13th January 1956:
A playgroup accident affects the lives of twin girls forever.
After all, there is no way to alter the past . . .
or is there?

Rosie McGrath travels back in time to 1956.
Can she survive that harsher world?
Will she be trapped there?
Can she change the events of that long-ago Friday
when her mother and aunt went their separate ways?

ISBN 1 85371 281 7

£4.99

Rosie's Quest by **Ann Carroll**
available from Poolbeg,
the *Irish* for bestsellers